THE GUNS OF GOBLIN VALLEY

ALSO BY JARRET KEENE

Kid Crimson Westerns

Gunpowder Mountain

THE GUNS OF GOBLIN VALLEY

A KID CRIMSON WESTERN
BOOK 2

JARRET KEENE

The Guns of Goblin Valley
Paperback Edition
Copyright © 2024 Jarret Keene

Wolfpack Publishing
1707 E. Diana Street
Tampa FL 33610

wolfpackpublishing.com

This book is a work of fiction. Any references to historical events, real people or real places are used fictitiously. Other names, characters, places and events are products of the author's imagination, and any resemblance to actual events, places or persons, living or dead, is entirely coincidental.

All rights reserved. No part of this book may be reproduced by any means without the prior written consent of the publisher, other than brief quotes for reviews.

Cover Illustration by Claudio Bergamin

Paperback ISBN 978-1-63977-615-3
eBook ISBN 978-1-63977-614-6
LCCN 2024940506

For Tony DeZuniga (1932-2012)

THE GUNS OF GOBLIN VALLEY

1

THE 3RD CALIFORNIA INFANTRY REGIMENT overstayed their welcome in Virginia City, having made camp at the base of Sun Mountain, far below the bustling board-walked streets of town, almost all the way down to the Carson River valley. Every morning, soldiers rudely stomped through the decrepit quarters of Paiute and Chinese residents before arriving in town to begin the day's tribunals. These informal trials were conducted in front of the First Presbyterian Church for the purpose of condemning Confederate spies and sympathizers who might be lurking in our mining town to the federal prison in Stockton, California. Most Johnny Reb supporters had lit out before the soldiers arrived, which frustrated them and inspired them to search harder.

Indeed, like all witch hunts, this one spiraled out of control.

My friend Chaparral, piano player at the Blood Nugget, got into a fistfight, cuffing three soldiers before being bayonet-slashed in the thigh outside his girlfriend Rosie's place on C Street. Apparently, someone had found out about her Mormon peepstone and told Colonel Connor. Connor hated Mormons, labeling them a plague of traitors, murderers, fanatics, and whores. He seemed to loathe them more than the Confederates he was supposed to remove from Virginia City. His vicious attitude toward Latter-day Saints, particularly the women, had incited a few of his soldiers to threaten to deport Rosie back to Salt Lake City, confiscate her cash register and bank accounts, and nationalize her business. Chaparral was the only musician I knew who had a background in bareknuckle boxing and street scrapping. He got in some pretty good licks.

Eventually, the soldiers overwhelmed Chaparral and had their fun, half-drowning him in a horse-watering trough and making him straddle a tall, sharp, wooden chevalet that they'd brought with them for torturing Indians and bandits. They began heating a pot of oil with the idea of tarring and feathering him, but ten-year-old Ezra, the shoeshine kid, had figured out their plan. He distracted them by walking up and shining their boots without asking, which gave his Paiute girlfriend Sarah, the animal wrangler, a chance to knock over the pot. For this, the kids were both rope-whipped once across the spine by a soldier named Ustick, after which they came running to find me as I'd been in the midst of busting up a brawl outside the livery. I wasn't the sheriff, but establishments paid me to keep the peace and to thwart drunks from damaging their businesses.

Ezra and Sarah told me everything, thinking I'd be upset over my friend's mistreatment. I was, but what really boiled my blood was that they'd been hurt. I'd been beaten plenty as a child by my own father, a cruel plantation owner. He'd hurt me enough so that I tended to get very mean when grown-ups struck youngsters.

As I made my way down C Street, I heard Ezra say to Sarah, "We shouldn't have told Crimson. He looks like he plans to kill all the soldiers."

"Too late now," she said. "I'll let Grover know to prepare some coffins."

I stopped to address them. "Not the undertaker. Get Poppy. Tell her to bring a rifle."

They sprinted toward Poppy's opium lounge, the Sure Cure. I resumed making my way to Rosie's.

After trying Chaparral for attempted murder against an officer of the United States in the middle of a road littered with animal droppings and windblown refuse, the soldiers tied his arms behind his back and placed him, bleeding from his leg, in a saddle atop a pinto. They tossed a rope over a lamppost and placed his head in a noose. Hair wet, face bloody, he gave no sign of fear, stoic in his cruel fate. Ustick, who'd earned most of Chaparral's punches, his eye swollen shut from the beating the piano player had laid on him, used his Union-blue forage cap to swat the horse's flank. Chaparral was left hanging.

Well, almost. I fired a bullet from my Colt Army Model 1860 single-action revolver that severed the rope in time to keep my friend's neck from snapping. He ended up remaining in the saddle, leaning forward against the mane of the pinto as it galloped down C Street.

The soldiers, jaws open, watched him escape.

Then they turned toward the source of the shot and saw me walking toward them, gun back in my holster, ready to draw it again and mow them down.

"Sir, you're interfering," Ustick said through a mouthful of busted teeth, "with official military business. You'll be tried for treason and executed."

"No," I said. "That won't happen today. Or ever."

One of the others nudged his brother-in-arms, and I heard my name hissed: *Crimson*.

I approached Ustick until our faces were inches apart. I calmly removed my black gaucho hat and smiled.

Then I viciously head-butted him, breaking his nose and causing him to fall backward into the dust with a groan as blood gushed from his nostrils.

With a Winchester in her gorgeous hands, Poppy stepped off the wooden sidewalk that ran along the storefronts. Her raven-black hair done up in a high bun, she wore a yellow embroidered silk dragon robe and wicker slippers, a vision of lethal beauty in a landscape of mining waste and human rapacity. She leveled the rifle at the other soldiers to discourage them from interrupting my intent to make a point. I detected Ezra and Sarah at the edge of the crowd that had gathered to watch me confront the Army.

"Y'all gonna die for this," a soldier warned, spitting at the ground.

"Kid," Clemens the newspaperman said, observing my wrath even as he scribbled into a notepad. "You're giving me too far much to write about here in a single article. Somehow, I sense a series in the works. Continue, please."

I laughed. Samuel Clemens, arch reporter for the *Territorial Enterprise*, had a sense of humor I found irresistible and oddly pacifying. He knew how to reduce my white-hot rage and saved Ustick several broken bones and a concussion or two.

I walked over to Clemens in an effort to account for myself, but again his wit was too quick. "I'd shake your hand, Crimson, but the Billy Yank's face seems to have reached it before I could."

"We simply put our heads together," I said.

Even the soldiers, Poppy's gun still trained on them, guffawed.

Colonel Connor came trotting up on his buckskin quarter horse, displeased with the tableau. He looked angry as he processed the details.

Always astute, Poppy propped the gun on her shoulder, cocked her hip, and smiled at the commander.

"Colonel, I have good news to share with our readers," Clemens said. "An unnecessary lynching was avoided today in Virginia City, thanks to the Kid."

"Wonderful, but can someone explain why," Connor said, "one of my men is on the ground, bleeding and crying and covered in his own blood?"

"The piano player socked Ustick," a soldier said. "So we tried the musician for attempted murder. Before we could string him up, Kid Crimson intervened. He and the Chinese girl should hang, sir. Maybe this newspaper poof too."

"Well, now *that*," Clemens said to Connor, ignoring the soldier's insinuation, "is a *lot* of hanging. Have you enough rope for exterminating so many good citizens of Virginia City, sir?"

"I have more than enough, Mr. Clemens," Connor said. "For your town and for devious butternuts like Crimson here. He has the scent of traitorous Georgia on him."

I said nothing. He was right about my birth state. I'd left the red clay of my home to seek infamy and fortune in Virginia City as a hired gun. I was doing well out here, with the aim of making enough to buy a grapefruit farm in Sonoma County. The sooner the better too, since my line of work was risky. The chances of perishing in a hail of bullets, or with my head in a noose, were good. I wouldn't die today though. Today my papers were in order.

"I'm in Virginia City to secure work, Colonel," I said finally, reaching into my jacket for a letter of transit. "I do jobs for Lincoln's adherents, like this man's brother." I indicated the newspaperman. "You may know Orion Clemens, Secretary of the Territory of Nevada."

I handed the document to Connor, who stayed mounted. He was a short man, no taller than five-foot-four, so I understood why he didn't square off with me in this circumstance. He studied the paper for a minute, and I noticed his eyes didn't move across the page. He was illiterate.

"Crimson, I'm not impressed," he said, handing the document back to me. "I've heard it said that you lost the president's body double in an air balloon mishap weeks ago."

I shrugged. "Can't save them all, sir."

"Well, I must admit that you succeeded in smoking out bushwhackers and copperheads. It could be argued that you helped lay the groundwork for what we've accomplished here."

"What *have* you accomplished exactly?" I said. "My poor friend, Chaparral, the piano player, has no warmth for the Confederacy. Yet your men antagonize him and his girlfriend."

Connor's horse gave a loud sigh, puncturing my complaint. "His girlfriend is a Mormon, I'm told. Witch-harlot with a crystal ball."

"It's a seer stone, sir. And Rosie is no prostitute. She's a good woman, excommunicated from her denomination for daring to challenge its orthodoxies."

"I didn't know. Perhaps there's hope for her."

"In any case, this document, signed by the Secretary

of Nevada," I said, returning it to my coat pocket, "makes it clear that my friends and I are to be left alone."

"Even the fey newspaperman?" one of the soldiers said, disappointed.

"That's the Secretary's brother, idiot," Connor responded.

"Far be it from me to insist on journalist protections." Clemens chuckled. "After all, advertisements contain the only truths to be relied on in a newspaper. But I wonder, Colonel Connor, when it is you plan on concluding your tribunals."

The commander opened his mouth to answer, but then there was the sound of a galloping horse approaching at full speed. Around the corner poor Chaparral came rocketing, still saddled on the spirited pinto, still with his hands tied behind his back, and still leaning forward to keep his balance. The animal's unkempt mane fluttered against his disheveled face. The horse and the piano player blasted past us, heading straight for Sun Mountain at incredible speed, dust flying.

Brow furrowed, Connor glared at his men and then at me, as if expecting one or all of us to resolve the issue of the runaway horse ridden by a sentenced musician. When none of us moved, he rubbed his beard with exasperation.

"I, Colonel Patrick Connor," he said for the benefit of the Virginia City press, "Commander of the 3rd California Infantry Regiment, officially announce the end of the tribunals here in Virginia City. My regiment leaves for Utah in the morning to direct our attention to the growing Indian problem."

Clemens wrote it all down in his notepad before asking, "What of the piano player, sir?"

"The degenerate musician's conviction is hereby overturned," Connor said. He brushed dust from his uniform as his men tended to Ustick, leading the shattered bastard to his horse for the ride back to camp. "Chaparral is free to go and will not be aggravated by my men, as long as he promises not to snipe us on our way out of the Comstock Lode."

"I can't speak for Chaparral," I said. "But I assure you he's in no condition to do anything except sit at a piano and play, with maudlin energy, 'Bonnie Blue Flag' as your regiment exits the valley."

Connor nodded at this, then peered at me with interest. "Why not join us, Crimson? We can use a warrior like you on the frontier against the savages that threaten our nation."

"Plenty of savagery here in Virginia City, Colonel. Why seek something that's before my eyes?"

"Good point. I trust you to keep this town in line, Crimson. The world changes, and men like us are all that stands in the way of it being overrun by villains."

"Yes," I said to him. "I will stand in the way, just as I know you do, sir."

Clemens nearly wrote it all down with a straight face.

2

SARAH, THE PRETERNATURAL PAIUTE GIRL, HAD settled the pinto by the time I reached the farm operated by Poppy's uncle John John, swineherd and restaurateur. John John had long sought to enlist Sarah to work in his slaughterhouse because of the way she befriended and bewitched animals, from half-feral hogs to whiptail lizards to sharp-shinned hawks. John John was, like most businessmen, oblivious to the trauma that empathic souls suffer in a world of destruction. He thought he might bend Sarah to his will, but she was a girl with a tricky, charismatic spark. If she went to work for John John, she'd have him grunting in the mud like one of his pigs.

"I was worried for the piano player at first," he said to me as I tethered my Appaloosa. "So I sent for Dr. Scullard."

"Scully is a drunken sawbones," I said. "You know better, John John."

He shrugged, picking up a bag of chicken feed. "Last week, Scully removed, from one of my pigs, the longest tapeworm I've seen on three continents." A former Manchu diplomat, John John had lived in China and England before making his way to the American West as a railroad worker.

"His degree is in veterinary medicine," I said. "Scully practices on humans here in Virginia City, because no one else has a background in human medicine."

"I knew nothing about food until I arrived in Virginia City. Did *you* provide security, Kid, in Georgia, before showing up in these streets?"

"You got me there, John John. Where is Chap, anyway?"

"Sarah and Rosie are with him now in my house, and he's responding well."

"Mind if I take a peek?"

John John gestured that I should head over, then began feeding the chickens as they clucked and pecked hungrily at the ground.

I made my way to John John's clapboard structure, illuminated within by hanging lanterns. I could hear laughter—Chaparral and Rosie. It stirred feelings inside me, my heart aching for my dearest Poppy. Days before the air balloon fiasco, which nearly resulted in me and Ezra getting ourselves killed by a Confederate schemer, I'd asked her, in bed, to run away with me to California to tend a grapefruit orchard. Her response was cold, and it hurt.

Propped up against the headboard of John John's bed, a bare-chested Chaparral looked to be in good spirits despite the bruises on his body, smiling and telling jokes. Rosie had tears of happiness in her eyes. Sarah, meanwhile, did her best to dab Chap's slashed leg with a mercurochrome-soaked cloth.

"Kid," he said, stretching out his arms but not standing to greet me. "You saved me again, brother."

"Next time you take on Colonel Connor and his Stockton boys," I said, removing my hat, "make sure Jericho and I are standing with you." Jericho was the roughneck bartender at the Blood Nugget, where Chaparral played piano. "You almost got your musical neck fermata-ed."

His expression went serious. "They insulted Rosie, Kid." He reached for her hands, gazing into his beloved's face as he spoke. "She's everything to me, and they had no right."

"Darling," she said. "They were baiting you."

"And you took the bait," I said to Chaparral. "Harder than a channel catfish in Washoe Lake."

He chuckled, then flinched when Sarah applied antiseptic. "Ouch!"

The ten-year-old girl returned his scowl. "You're a big baby."

"That's a bayonet wound. Ever been sliced by a drunk soldier, little girl?"

"I watched soldiers kill my mother."

Chaparral got quiet after that, reaching for Sarah's shoulder by way of apology.

She dropped the cloth and darted out of John John's home. I considered running after her, but I'd learned to give Sarah space when she was vexed.

"Well, I'm a fool," Chaparral said.

"I'll talk to her," Rosie said. "You didn't mean anything. She knows you care and want to keep her safe."

He nodded. "Safety. Kid, before Connor's men came after me, I overheard something."

"I already know," I said. "Connor is headed to Utah to

wipe out the Indians. There's nothing we can do about it, Chap."

"Hang on, there's more. They're searching for a steelworks operation."

"What? Where?"

"Goblin Valley, Utah."

"Come on, Chap, there's no reason for a factory out in the middle of nowhere."

"Telling you what I heard."

"So who's building it?"

"Mormons, I imagine."

"Makes sense," Rosie said. "After Joseph Smith's murder in Carthage, the Saints have been amassing weapons, including cannons."

"You're suggesting," I said, "that they're constructing a munitions plant in Goblin Valley."

"I'm not suggesting anything. Once my nerves are quelled, I can consult my stone." Rosie had a mystic peepstone that she gazed into which provided her glimpses of the near future. The images were always intriguing, and sometimes useful—if you managed to decipher what the images meant.

"I know how to soothe you, Rosie," Chaparral said, starting to push himself out of bed until he groaned in pain, realizing he wasn't ready. "On second thought, that torture horse left a mark."

"Poor Chappy," she cooed, brushing her fingers against his bare chest.

"I'll confer with Ralston on the steelworks," I said, donning my hat to indicate I was leaving. "If there's action in Utah, he'll know about it."

"Tell Sarah I'm sorry for whining so much. Tell her thanks for stopping the horse."

"She'll be okay. Takes more than an ivory-tickler to upset her for long."

Chaparral nodded. "You're the best, Kid."

"Take the night off. I'm sick of hearing Chopin anyway. I prefer 'Oh Shenandoah.'"

"I'll play it all night long tomorrow, if I'm well enough."

"Sounds delightful." I left him alone with Rosie tending to him.

Outside, I found Sarah feeding an apple to King Zhou, the largest of John John's gunpowder-sniffing pigs. She had a bright smile, which I didn't wish to dampen by mentioning Chap's apology.

Her smile evaporated anyway when Dr. Mortimer Scullard approached. He stumbled on uneven slush as he pulled from his unfastened medical bag a stethoscope. He stooped to apply the device's rubber bell to the spine of King Zhou, busily chewing an apple core.

Sarah looked on with fascination as Scully, breathing heavily from the liquor and from the strain required in bending over to listen to a pig's internal body sounds, conducted his diagnosis.

Finally, he was done and said to her as if she were the caretaker, "This creature is in perfect health. Keep her out of the poisonous mines, and she'll live a long, productive life."

Sarah then offered Scully an apple, which he waved away with a mumbling noise.

He shoved the stethoscope back into the bag, failing to zip it closed completely, and trudged back to his carriage.

By this time, John John had walked over to observe the doctor struggling to pull himself into the seat and secure the reins.

"John John," I said. "What did you do with the pig from which Scully removed the tapeworm?"

"Sold it to Colonel Connor's men for a dollar. I believe they spit-roasted it in their camp." He pressed against one side of his nose to loudly blast a wad of snot into the sludge.

Startled by this noise and everything she'd seen so far, Sarah looked up at me. "This isn't a good place for animals, Crimson Boy."

"Worse for people," I said.

The next morning, as the 3rd California Infantry Regiment headed out of Virginia City on a mission to exterminate Indians, I breakfasted with Ralston, banking and investor extraordinaire, who had a stranglehold it seemed, on all mining operations at the Comstock Lode and beyond. He paid me handsomely to do dangerous jobs, which I relished to my own confusion. On the one hand, I dreamed of California. On the other, I took pleasure in conducting aggressive security operations for Ralston. It wasn't money that validated me; it was knowing that I could inflict sanctioned violence against a world that had tried, unsuccessfully, to snuff me. Starting with my deranged father who never met a slave that he didn't viciously whip.

Or a mixed-race son.

Ralston and I met at my favorite nook, the Griddle of Doom. Over cinnamon pancakes and black coffee, we talked about the pointlessness of tribunals and the ongoing fallout from the air balloon mishap. Ralston was as garrulous as ever, but I sensed that he had information burning in his brain, something he longed to tell me. I could detect that he wondered if I still trusted him given the omission of sensitive details during the last job that he'd given me. Namely that the President Lincoln that had visited Virginia City wasn't really Lincoln at all, but a body double used to smash a Confederate plot.

"What's in the past is done," I said, allaying his concern. "I look forward to collaborating with you, mining superintendent John Mackay, and Verbena at the Blood Nugget to keep Virginia City free and clear of malicious conspiracies."

My ploy seemed to work as he took a pen and some paper from his jacket. He drew what looked like a symbol or a badge—a wheel with an eight-pointed star in the center.

"Recognize this?" he said.

"Of course," I said. "It's the sign of the Knights of the Golden Circle."

"So you know what they do? Their aims?"

I sighed louder than I'd intended. "My father was a member. Perhaps he still is. The Golden Circle is a secret society determined to enlarge the Southern United States, expand slavery, and assassinate Lincoln and any and all abolitionists throughout the Americas. The organization has designs on Mexico, Cuba, Haiti, and so on."

"I didn't know that," Ralston said. "About your father."

I didn't want to reveal anything more. "Why bring up the knights?"

"As the war intensifies, this nefarious cartel is exploring its options in the Southwest. There are sympathizers everywhere, even amid the Mormons."

"That's because the federal government has persecuted the Latter-day Saints relentlessly, along with the Indians."

Ralston displayed annoyance whenever I pointed out historical context. "Sure, but there's ill-gotten gold, likely stolen from Mexico, being pushed into Nevada, Arizona, and Utah. Some of it seems to be funding gun factories and powder mills west of Texas. Why? Brass cannons of the Confederacy are being outclassed by the Union's field-howitzers that fire twelve-pound cannonballs. So now the South is seeking a location to forge its own heavy armament."

"Funny that you and I are discussing this. I spoke with Chaparral yesterday—"

"Heard he got into a scrap with Connor's men. How's he doing?"

"Chap is healing up fine. What I was going to say was that Chap claims he overheard soldiers chewing over an aspect of their Utah trip. Something about steelworks in Goblin Valley."

"Yes, well, I can't imagine Brigham Young allowing Johnny Reb to set up operations that deep inside Utah. That all you got?"

"Ralston," I said, pushing my plate away, my hunger having ebbed. "Connor's regiment was here conducting tribunals because of you and, yes, your effective ploy to root out traitors to the Union cause. Now you're saying you don't know what the Army is up to?"

"Kid, don't get the wrong impression. I have the president's ear from time to time. But that doesn't mean we're in regular contact. Or that I'm privy to his directives. Connor could be getting marching orders from numerous people. I'm not one of them."

"I see where this is going," I said. "Or where *I'm* going."

"It's an easy assignment. Follow Connor's regiment

into Utah and see if there's anything to the Goblin Valley rumor."

I watched steam rising from my coffee cup. Then I picked up the mug and sipped.

"You'll consider it, I hope," Ralston said, smirking.

"I'm considering. Why not have Colonel Connor report to you?"

"He thinks he reports to Lincoln alone. And let's face it, his hatred of Mormons blinds him, prevents him from being a functional officer."

"Can't you ask Lincoln's man, Orion Clemens, to ship Connor to the South to, I don't know, burn farmland?"

"I doubt Connor can strike a lucifer match. I need you to monitor and report back."

I thought about it more, and it hit me. "Ralston, there's a lot of ore-processing happening at the moment on Ophir Hill. Any chance you're looking to move some of that equipment from Goblin Valley into Virginia City to enhance your investments?"

He wiggled a toothpick between his front teeth. "Kid, I'm only interested in doing what's right."

"I need to bring Bad Jace. If he stays here, he'll cause havoc."

Ralston didn't appreciate Bad Jace for the simple reason that the outlaw had his own agenda and a penchant for wanton, unpredictable cruelty. I, of course, found Bad Jace to be highly useful in desperate situations that called for extreme, even fiendish, measures. I was also beginning to learn more about his surprising erudition, uncanny serenity, and inscrutable motivation. For the sake of my Virginia City friends, Bad Jace was someone I needed to puzzle out, and the best way to do that was on the trail.

"I'll give you money to pay him," Ralston said.

I nodded, extended my hand for a gentleman's agreement, which he accepted. "I'll need a few things at House of Hammers."

"Your account there remains open. How are things with the girl, Kid?" Despite my affection for Poppy, Ralston had seen me kiss Verbena when we were all in the air balloon weeks ago. I was sure he meant the beautiful Chinese opium purveyor, but perhaps he was needling me.

"Things are ideal," I said. "They'll be even better once I've amassed enough dollars to exit Virginia City."

"I think you like it here, Kid. You clearly relish the pancakes."

"Thanks for breakfast, Ralston. Hey, one more question."

"Give it to me."

"Am I working for you this time or the US government?"

"You're working for *all* of us, Kid. And you have our complete support."

"I hope that remains true this time, sir. Falling off an exploding mountain and miraculously landing atop an air balloon has left me feeling a bit, well, forsaken."

3

EZRA CAME RUNNING TO TELL ME, AND I HAD TO calm the impulse to yell at him. I watched him hurtle down the steep cross streets of town through dense, chaotic traffic, tumbling head over heels, threading the wheels of a wagon and then barely making it under a horse's belly going the other direction. Only a dozen kids lived in Virginia City; they were all cocksure, reckless, bellicose. Their only civilizing influence was Sunday church, which I abhorred. Grover dragged Ezra and Sarah to First Presbyterian when he could, hoping the lamb of God might rub off on these young lions. If anything, having to sit still for an hour made Ezra and Sarah even more merciless in their conduct. Children didn't benefit from living in a contentious boomtown. Then again, I was raised on a lavish plantation—with horses, private tutors, finery, my own slaves—and I nearly paid for it with my life. My mother had died as a result of my father's violent streak and lust for treasure. In any case, I didn't raise my voice at Ezra. I'd promised myself to never berate him due to my experience as a Georgia scion.

"That was a close call," I said. "Please be careful or you'll end up in one of Grover's coffins."

"Miners have surrounded Verbena," he said, out of breath. "She needs help, Kid!"

I'd intended to pick up a few items at House of Hammers and leave that afternoon, but the departure of Connor's regiment stirred emotions in Virginia City. To our town's credit, very few if any had informed on friends and neighbors during the tribunals, mainly because Connor was an incompetent inquisitor. Another reason was that the primary Confederate plotter, Grinaker, had been smoked out and killed, suggesting to everyone that Johnny Reb was no longer a threat. Once Connor rode away though, a cluster of Dead Dice patrons grew ornery. They'd lost money gambling before Grinaker died, and believed they were owed compensation. In their view, a traitor to the Union was obviously scamming customers. They showed up looking for refunds.

It wasn't going to happen. Verbena was the Dead Dice's new owner, having arranged for me to defend her property from all threats. Not everyone knew about the change in ownership, or about my services extending to the Dead Dice. And no one knew that I cared for Verbena in ways I wasn't ready to acknowledge. They'd find out soon enough.

A quintet of dusty, desperate miners had barged in and broken some furniture. Jericho was tending at the Blood Nugget, unaware that his boss was surrounded by ruffians hoping to intimidate her into opening the register. Verbena didn't have a gun, choosing to smash a bottle and hold them off with a fistful of jagged glass.

When I walked into the Dead Dice, I saw that two of them had grabbed a length of curtain fabric from the windows, intending to tangle her up so they could slap her around.

"Spirited bitch," one of them said.

"Pay us what we're owed," another growled.

"What you'll get," Verbena hissed, "is your face sliced open." The puff sleeve of her saloon dress had slipped off her shoulder, revealing a cleavage almost from her neck to her bellybutton, and she looked ravishing when poised to cause injury. Or maybe I admired her capacity to commit violence against those who deserved it.

The men with the drapery charged, snarling her in red velvet and knocking her off her feet.

Before they put their dirty hands on her, the monster inside me was unleashed.

I grabbed the chubby one by the arm and used my Bowie knife to skewer-nail his wrist to a support column. His screams of agony caused the other one to turn, and I had a chair ready to smash him over the head. He didn't get up.

The three remaining miners hesitated, which was a mistake.

I'd smithereened the chair against their friend's skull, but the wooden stile remained in my grip. I whipped it across the teeth of another ingrate, his blood splashing the eyes of the man beside him. Then I boot-stomped the kneecap of the mouth-lashed miner, putting him down. His friend wiped gore from his vision in time to catch my fist with his chin, which sent him crashing into a faro table, playing cards fluttering in the air. He was knocked out cold.

The fifth miner went running for the batwing doors. But Jericho had heard there was mayhem occurring. He grabbed the miner by the throat and choked him into submission.

For the fight's duration—maybe thirty seconds—the first miner, whose hand I'd impaled, never ceased screaming. He finally yanked the knife free, but when he studied the blade and saw blood pouring from his wound, he gasped and keeled over from sheer fright.

I pulled Verbena free of the heavy fabric and inspected her for signs of injury. She was lovely, and as I brushed the dust from her dress, she giggled at the outcome of this absurd fracas.

"Kid," she said, "you're worth every penny."

She moved to kiss me. I should've demurred, but the monster hadn't yet crawled back into his cage. I took her in my arms passionately and savored her delicious mouth.

"Um, boss?" Jericho said, headlocking the one who tried to escape. "What do I do here?"

Verbena walked up to him, peering under her bartender's armpit. She said to the grimacing miner, "Sir, your gang's effort to extort from me was uncalled for. This bar is under new management now, and I'm not responsible for the previous owner's shenanigans."

"New proprietor?" the man whimpered. "Since when? We didn't know that. Why didn't nobody tell us? Why didn't *you* tell us?"

"You didn't really give me the chance."

"We...we just thought...that you...hell, life is totally upside down around here! With those damn bluebellies in town, drinking all the whiskey and monopolizing the women and asking so many questions, it's been a confusing existence. We almost prefer life in the hole over a night in Virginia City. Why, the only entertainment we've taken in for weeks is the circus over by Boot

Hill. Clowns and peanuts and trapeze artists are fine, but not the same as a robust saloon girl."

I could see Verbena considering this. She made the right call as always. Miners lived in constant fear of death—from fire, cave-ins, and seeping gases. They, more than anyone, were entitled to a good time.

"Take your friends to see Dr. Scullard. Tell him I'm paying the bill. When you're patched up, come back here. I'll set you up with a round of drinks. We'll move forward with the shared understanding that the Dead Dice and the Blood Nugget are the best places for men like you to enjoy yourselves and pursue your vices. In fact," she said, grabbing a whiskey bottle from the bar top and extending it, "start with this."

Jericho instantly released the miner, who looked surprised that he was free to go and had been offered gratis booze. He took the bottle and said, without making eye contact, "Thank you, ma'am." Then he and the one I'd cuffed into a faro game gathered their busted-up buddies and left to find Scully. They shambled off slowly, as I'd administered a larruping.

Verbena, Jericho, and I swept the floor, tossing pieces of broken furniture into the trash.

After we tidied up the Dead Dice, she said, "Did you know about the circus?"

I shrugged. "One came through last year. Ralston and Mackay pay to offset any losses accrued from producing a show in the Nevada wasteland. The circus admits Chinese and Paiute citizens at a reduced price, too. My sense is that the ringmaster pitches the big top beside Boot Hill to blunt the Washoe zephyrs that swoop down through Eagle Valley."

"Years ago, I heard a wild tale, Kid," Verbena said, "about a circus that maneuvered across the desert

Southwest, leaving a plague of violent death in its wake."

"Ha, well, I don't think this is the same circus. Although Ezra maintains that there's a fat man, big as a buggy, who doesn't stop eating boiled ears of corn. If he's large enough, I may hire him to assist me with security."

She smiled, then seemed to fret over whatever was irking her. "Can you find out when the circus is leaving? I have a bad feeling. Their choice of location still doesn't sit right."

"That they never drank at your bar galls you," I teased. "Should I buy us two tickets? I haven't seen flying trapeze artists since my childhood days in Georgia."

"I don't think Poppy would like that," Verbena said, drawing close, staring up at me with soulful eyes. She placed a French hairpin between her gorgeous lips as she raised her arms to pull her hair back and arrange it into a bun. Her pits were unshaven, and I wanted to inhale her like an animal. "You should take your fiancée."

"I should catch up with Connor. But I'll pause a moment to observe the circus for you."

"Don't run away with them, Kid. Or anyone else for that matter. No one pays as well as I do."

"Verbena, darling. I could never abandon you or this sideshow of a mining hamlet."

EZRA AND SARAH didn't miss any developments, having informed me of the arrival of the canvas-covered cages on wagons and the unloading of animals several days prior. Rather than ride the rails, the circus traveled on buckboard wheels and horse sweat. A small outfit,

Circus Southwest boasted tamed mustangs, an elephant, a lion, and a trapeze act of two lovely French sisters, plus a sideshow of so-called "human oddities," who seemed unscrupulous and prone to violence. Though I hadn't yet seen the circus show this time, I'd long admired Nellie Brown, a black knife-juggler. She tossed blades like a human thresher, her feet in the inner stirrups of two horses bolting at full speed in a wide circle under the big top. She was easy on the eyes, but I what I really coveted was her skill. I imagined her to be engrossing company.

There was a performance slated in the next thirty minutes, so I took a moment to chat with Grover the undertaker. Much to Poppy's exasperation, I continued to sleep most nights in the back of his coffin shop. I didn't know why I preferred gloomy quarters, but I suspected it was because I didn't plan on living long as a hired gun. I believed the way to get accustomed to death was to saw logs in a satin-lined pine box. Like Poppy, Grover considered my methods preposterous. Indeed, many of my beliefs made him scratch his head. Yet he loved me unconditionally. I loved him right back, wishing I could be a better surrogate son, since there was never a better proxy father than he was to me. I was shaped into the killer that stood before him. It was too late to save me, unless I managed to reach California.

"Kid," he said, reading under the shade of an umbrella-adorned bench that he'd built in front of Grover's Graveside Services. "I'm starting to think your exploits are less of a liability after all."

"That's because you haven't heard," I said, "about the dustup at the Dead Dice."

He stood up to embrace me, and I returned his affection. "I know about it. Ezra described every detail."

I looked around. "He still here?"

"Left early to see the circus. That boy loves elephants."

"What about his little Indian girlfriend?"

"Sarah? He bought her another ticket too. This is their fifth time seeing the circus together."

"I would've paid their admission. He should save his shoeshine money."

Grover shrugged. "Sometimes we spend on silly things for those we love."

I started to say that, growing up among Southern gentry, no one ever bought me trifles. I was taught to fight at age nine, a gun being the first gift my father gave me. But Grover suspected my grisly childhood, so there was no point in sharing. And I detected the truth in his words.

"What are you reading, Grover?"

He held up a dime novel, a pamphlet-length work with my name and likeness on it. The painted cover of *Dime Library* sported a slender man in black with a red cravat and a Sharps .50-cal rifle standing atop a mountain, an air balloon soaring into the sun.

"You're famous, Kid."

I rubbed my face with embarrassment, nearly knocking over my hat. "Where did you find that?"

"Ezra loves these books. He'll be thrilled by your fictionalized adventures. The news dealer has been slow, so I sent a dollar to New York for the latest." Rosie had taught Ezra to read.

"Did Clemens write it for quick money?"

"Come on, Kid, you know Clemens can't write like a Neanderthal. I'm debating whether I should frame this for the office."

"Please don't," I said, queasy from the attention. I preferred operating in relative obscurity. The notion that lewd scriveners in the Northeast had heard of me spiked my hackles. If they grew too curious, they might explore my past—and locate my father if he was still alive.

Grover noted my concern. "Don't worry, Kid," he said, sliding the book under a stack of periodicals. "Have a sense of humor about it. Besides, I read all the papers, from the *San Francisco Bulletin* to the *New York World*. I'll keep you abreast of how you're portrayed. You can continue reading your Emerson and Thoreau and remain oblivious to commercial prose."

That struck me as funny. "I appreciate it, Grover. Say, what do you think of the spot where the circus pitched its big top?"

"Not much. It's closer to the Chinese cemetery this year, I guess, but I heard that Ringmaster Clyde worked out a deal whereby everyone on E Street gets to the show at least once for free."

"Still servicing the Chinese?"

Grover nodded. "I don't make a point of telling people, but yes. Their money is as good as anyone else's. And the food they serve upon a grave? Even Colonel Connor loved it."

I refrained from telling him about the assignment Verbena gave me, not because I wished to keep him in the dark, but because I didn't know exactly why she was suspicious. "Let's have dinner when I return from Utah, Grover. Verbena always enjoys hosting you at the Blood Nugget.

"Sure, Kid. We'll do that. Enjoy the show. You'll run into Ezra and Sarah, I'm sure."

4

Ignoring superstition and decency, I took a shortcut through the Chinese cemetery, located on the other side of Boot Hill facing Sun Mountain. John John's farm was nearby, nestled within adjacent acreage in a pocket valley, a low area surrounded by steep ridges to the east and south. Nearly three hundred Chinese souls lived in Virginia City, and they were laid to rest in the cemetery if they didn't make it out. Since the whites were focused on mining and banking and lawyering and newspapering, they were incapable of doing laundry or preparing hog meat or even cooking for themselves. The Chinese provided these services. For a time, they'd also made good miners, until the Cornish and Irish immigrants and abiding distrust pushed them out.

I walked through the desolate space, devoid of flowers and headstones. The trees had all been chopped down for winter firewood. It was now a bare hillside, unpainted pieces of board lying flat and featuring Chinese calligraphy, the letters written in pencil, identifying the dead. Scattered on the ground were prayer papers, tossed to the wind by mourners during a procession. I noticed a number of fresh graves and began walking toward them to investigate.

"Crimson."

My heart suddenly filled with cheer and hope. I turned and saw her, stunning in a sleeveless floral burgundy keyhole dress. She approached, hands behind her back, the slit in her dress revealing her gorgeous legs. Her hair was done up in the Hanfu style, her long ponytail tied loosely so that the length framed her face on both sides, showcasing her flawless forehead. Her embroidered red pointed-toe flat shoes were adorable. I wanted to slip them off and eat her toes.

"Fancy finding you here, my love," I said. "Paying respects or following me?"

For the briefest moment, I thought she might be obscuring her jade-handled Derringer, primed to shoot me for running an errand for Verbena. The two women had an interesting history, and a friendship that was at times contentious, at others intriguingly Sapphic.

She presented me with a purple lilac bouquet. I took the flowers, and pressed them to my chest. "Poppy, what's the occasion?"

"Today is our anniversary," she said, smiling bashfully.

"So it is," I said, covering for my deplorable lapse. "I can't believe how quickly time has passed. Feels like we just met."

"A full year," she said, her lips wet and luscious, "is a long time, Kid."

"You still want to get married?"

She came in for a hug, pressing her cheek to my sternum. I loved how doll-like she felt in my arms, her body lithe and lovely.

"I'm ready to say yes. When will you ask me?"

"There are conditions."

"The grapefruit orchard?"

"That's one."

"Go on."

"Three sons."

"Including Ezra?"

I nodded.

"We can begin," she said, smiling and standing on her toes to kiss me in a cemetery, "fulfilling that request on our wedding night."

"Poppy," I said, stepping away. "Come away with me."

"Kid, my business is here in Virginia City."

"It's an opium establishment, my flower."

"I'm helping these men. They're wounded by war, by nearly dying underground."

"You can't save them. But you can save *me*."

She crossed her arms. Her eyes displayed no resentment. She was pondering my words.

"You're not cut out for farming, Kid," she said. "Besides, you're leaving tonight to follow Connor's regiment. Ralston offers you terrible jobs. And you always accept them."

"I need money to buy an orchard."

"That's your excuse. You need violence the way men in the Sure Cure need opium."

I couldn't respond. Her observation was a punch to my stomach.

"I don't want to fight with *you*," I said.

"Then let's not."

God, how I wanted to kiss her. "I have to check on something before I light out."

"Ah, you're doing *that* job for Verbena."

I nodded, trying not to appear guilty. "I know you prefer the opera house, my flower, but—"

"Take me to the circus, Kid, and buy me popcorn."

I held out my arm. She slid her delicate hand around it.

We traversed a gravescape, her head on my shoulder as we went toward the cacophony—trumpeting elephants, barking ringmaster, shrill calliope, and much applause and laughter.

RINGMASTER CLYDE'S Circus Southwest was riotous, ridiculous. Under the big top, Clyde strutted in his tasseled top hat with gold buttons and his black leather boots, a masculine, handlebar-mustachioed presence, red coattails flapping behind him like flags in a gale. Meanwhile, his pretty-in-pink ballet dancers were deliciously flamboyant, otherworldly; the women conducted swift movements—pirouette, plié, *en pointe*—in tight, knitted-cotton leotards and ballet shoes, as Clyde's booming, bullhorn-powered voice cut through the noise of a Saturday afternoon crowd. He announced the epic history of each act in detail—how, for instance, the lion tamer learned the science of animal psychology from ancestors who dated as far back as in the catacombs of ancient Rome, where Emperor Nero had fed Christians to half-starved beasts. All the while the calliope kept churning its metallic, melodic fanfare as spectators chewed candy apples, fry cakes, and boiled peanuts.

I was pleased and not surprised to see Ezra and Sarah sitting right up front. She was throwing popcorn into his mouth, and he made dramatic faces as he caught each one and chewed crazily. For all their hardscrabble lives in a mining boomtown, it was a delight to catch a glimpse of their innocence, laughing in the wooden bleachers, anticipation crackling through the air like a static charge; two simple children dazzled by the colorful, animal-scented artifice of a traveling circus show.

I envied them. When I was their age, my father served *me* up as entertainment for evil men, scum of the earth who enjoyed watching children hurt one another in a pit. As Poppy and I took our seats, I began to realize the circus, with its brutal treatment of animals, wasn't much different from the kid-fight circuit in the South, a revolting spectacle spawned from hell. I could feel my hands begin to shake, sweat emanating in the gap between my shoulder blades.

"Kid," Poppy said. "You okay?"

The lion tamer's whip cracked, and I flinched. A memory suppurated inside my mind. I saw the enslaved woman, Hanna, whom I loved with all my heart, tied to a whipping post, the torment on her face as my father beat her unconscious, the male slaves holding me down and making me watch on my knees, red clay on my wet face turning into mud the color of blood.

"I'm fine," I said. "I'll get us a beer."

I signaled to a man selling snacks and German-style lagers from a barrel strapped to his back. He pulled two glasses from a wicker basket that he'd been carrying by a handle. He wiped the glasses with a rag, then turned the spigot on the barrel, releasing the golden-colored beer into each vessel and handing them to me. I gave him fifty cents and waved away the change. It was, no doubt, a bigger tip than he'd seen all day.

"Let me know what else I can get you, sir!"

I gave him another quarter. "What's the itinerary for Circus Southwest?"

The man, a beefy Scot, scanned the big top, as if someone might be watching. "You didn't hear it from me, but tonight Ringmaster Clyde is moving us to Utah. We've squeezed everything we can from Virginia City."

I looked around. The bleachers thronged with drunk miners, mid-level bank managers, Chinese workers, even a stray Paiute or two. "Seems like business is bustling."

He shrugged. "There's a string of towns from Dayton to Salt Lake City. Clyde insists these will fill our coffers, setting us up for a cozy winter."

"You'll be following in the wake of Colonel Connor's regiment."

"The Union boys? Soldiers don't make enough to warrant seeing our show. Unless they start earning better pay, they're of no interest to Circus Southwest."

That wasn't what I was suggesting. What I meant was that the 3rd California Infantry Regiment's Indian-killing mission didn't benefit the circus. To bring up the rear on a series of random, roaming atrocities with a caravan of animals and acrobats didn't seem like a good idea.

"Thank you," I said, dropping another coin into the vendor's meaty palm.

"Enjoy the show, sir!" He tipped his cap and scaled the bleachers, hollering his beer pitch.

Poppy felt my forehead. "Kid, you're clammy."

The whip continued to crack. The animals moved resentfully, under duress. I pondered my own bestial nature, how I'd lashed out at everyone in Georgia before stealing a horse and hitting the trail to Texas. "I told you I'm fine."

"I see Sarah intently studying the animals," Poppy said. "Think she'll behave?"

I hadn't considered that, my mind on far too many other things. Leave it to Poppy to worry about the girl.

Sarah had an uncanny bond with all of God's creatures. I suspected she was troubled by the exploitation of animals. But she was clearly enjoying the event, next to her shoeshiner boyfriend.

Then, before I could reply, the lovely Nellie Brown appeared in the spotlight, walking to the center of the ring in a two-tone blue silk faille dress, her bodice front adorned with couched silk threads spangled with brass beads. Arms raised, she held three knives by the blades in each hand. Instead of the calliope ringing out, a formally trained cellist—not some low-rent catgut-scraper—seated near the trapeze ladder began playing Bach's "Cello Suite No.1 in G major," a favorite of Chaparral's.

The gas lights dimmed, the crowd hushed, all of us caught in the suspenseful moment just before a woman flipped razor-sharp death above her head.

She made it look easy, tossing knives into the air, catching them, and tossing them again as if she were born the Queen of Blades. As the cellist confidently churned out resonant arpeggios and a comforting countermelody, Nellie kept her knives moving from hand to hand, at least four always suspended, her neck craned and sensually vulnerable as she studied the way each blade fell back into her catch-and-release possession.

"Wow," Poppy said, impressed. "What concentration."

"Sure," I said, "but can she throw with precision?"

As if overhearing me, Nellie turned toward a large spinning Wheel of Death, a classic moving target stunt prop that the acrobats had pushed into the ring, ten yards from where she stood. Ringmaster Clyde stepped out of the darkness and removed his tuxedo-style jacket, hanging it on a conveniently placed coat rack. Then the acrobats fastened his limbs to the wheel with leather straps and began spinning him slowly, the wooden frame of the wheel creaking.

Nellie threw six knives at Clyde. Each blade *thunk*-ing into the wheel caused a wave of anxiety to ripple across the bleachers. She landed the knives inches from Clyde's body, the last one striking between his legs, perilously close to his family jewels.

The applause was thunderous. Nellie took a bow as the acrobats helped Clyde off the wheel.

"I need her for this mission," I said.

Poppy pouted, crossed her arms. "That all you need her for?"

I just couldn't figure her. Jealous, possessive, and needy on the one hand, fiercely protective of her business, career, and independence on the other. What was a guy to do—except say something stupid. "Perhaps she has a passion for *pamplemousse*," I said, using the French term for grapefruit, which Poppy considered pretentious and pompous.

She tossed the rest of her beer in my lap and left me sitting in a puddle.

I was using my handkerchief to soak up what I could when I saw Bad Jace approaching, tall and menacing. He'd been bathing more regularly in recent weeks, soap and water making his presence almost tolerable. He remained a mean old cuss, snatching a candied apple from the hands of an eight-year-old sitting next to Ezra. As the boy burst into tears, Bad Jace chewed it down in a few bites, tossed the stick over his shoulder, and wiped his mouth with his hand. When he reached my place in the bleachers, he turned to look back at the kids. He laughed as Sarah gave him the finger.

"Your date," he said to me, "didn't go well, Kid."

"Did Verbena tell you where I was?"

He nodded. "Ran into Ralston too. Looks like you and I are tracking Connor to Goblin Valley."

"Yes, but first we should pick up some ammunition at Roscoe's House of Hammers."

"Already done."

I looked at him and saw that his expression was tense. "Something troubling you?"

"I'm eager to get moving. Sitting still in Virginia City has worn out my nerves. There's not a single card-player in town that I don't want to punctuate with bullets."

I recognized the feeling. We left the big top as the trapeze act got underway, and I had to admit that, despite my skin crawling in Bad Jace's presence, a part of me yearned to hit the trail with him. Leaving Virginia City meant new scenarios of mayhem. The monster inside me had bristled for too long under the soft management of Colonel Connor's regiment. I was curious to know what kind of munitions the Mormons were building in Goblin Valley.

On our way to the livery, I made the mistake of following instead of leading Bad Jace. He took us through the cemetery and we ended up walking across the resting places of a dozen or more men that I'd killed since arriving in Virginia City.

He noticed his misnavigation. "Sorry, Kid."

"Don't give it a second thought, Bad Jace. Sometimes you must confront your handiwork."

"Ghosts don't stay buried though."

I ignored his comment. "Say, any idea about that cluster of fresh graves in the Chinese cemetery? Grover didn't mention them."

"No," he said. "However, I seem to recall a tale about a gang that hid loot inside a coffin."

"You think someone stashed his silver there?"

Bad Jace laughed. "I'm not itching to find out. That place is haunted."

"You *do* believe in specters."

He stopped in his tracks to give me a hard look. "Let's change the subject."

I nodded, and we kept moving.

"Bad Jace fears the supernatural," I said, unable to help myself.

"Kid," he said. "I see now why women pour beer on you."

I tossed the lilacs Poppy had given me on an unmarked grave.

5

We loaded up on ammunition at House of Hammers, a hardware store on C Street that served as a gun shop. Virginia City residents and miners bought their lumber, tools, and weapons there. The owner, Roscoe, somehow managed to secure anything I needed. If Roscoe didn't have it in stock, he'd telegraph a distributor in Chicago or San Francisco. A week later, whatever I'd requested arrived by train and was in my violent hands. When I told him I could use a range of knives for throwing at targets, he didn't bat an eye. He pulled out a hardtack crate full of blades—mostly kitchen knives that Roscoe had sharpened for mining-camp cooks.

"These will nick you if you're not careful," he said. "I had your girlfriend's cousin, Sing, grind them to a razor's edge."

I skipped a beat at the word "girlfriend," unsure as always about Poppy and me, but I let it pass. "This one is unusual," I said, pulling from the clatter what looked like a long-bladed thrusting dagger. It gleamed in the light streaming through the window.

"Scottish dirk," Roscoe said. "A fighting dagger that's not designed for throwing, but someone with enough skill can make it work, I reckon. There's a few in the box."

"I know someone who will love this."

Roscoe squinted. "I see you're still doing jobs with that Bad Jace fellow."

"Sometimes you need a real bastard on your side when things go sideways."

"Well, make sure," he said, "Bad Jace ain't the reason."

Out of habit, I reached for my wallet.

"Go on now," he said. "This is on Ralston's bill."

I lifted the crate from the counter. "Thanks, Roscoe. I appreciate the knives."

"Pincushion someone who has it coming."

"Need anything from Utah?"

"A stout bride. I hear those Mormon fellows have more women than they know what to do with in their plural marriages." Roscoe's late wife had died from diphtheria during a trip to California three years ago.

"I'll see what I can rustle."

He chuckled. "Be safe out there, Kid."

"Always, Roscoe."

Bad Jace had loaded the wagon with ammo and victuals. It was the same carriage we'd driven on our way back to Virginia City from Rattlepeak.

"My derrière hurts just from looking at this wagon," I said, loading the crate of blades.

"Well, your *face* must hurt, too Kid. It's killing me."

"One to talk, Bad Jace. We need to stop by the circus."

"You can't get enough of that lion."

"I'm recruiting."

"Kid, you'll need Sarah if you plan on bringing an animal. But that won't work either, because I'm not riding with wild beasts or Sarah again."

"Relax," I said, hopping into the driver's box. "You'll love my idea."

Bad Jace harrumphed. "I've got that hand-cranked gun you requested. It's under the tarp."

"We have the correct rounds?"

"We do," he said, pulling himself into the buckboard as I snapped the reins.

I didn't know how he'd react to what I'd planned with regards to Nellie, so I thought it best to let him deal with it in the moment. I didn't want to hear any complaints beforehand, and I knew something about Bad Jace that most didn't. He loved surprises, especially dangerous ones. They gave him the freedom to react with savage abandon and cunning lethality. It's why he routinely walked into saloons where he knew he'd encounter raving lunatics begging for a whupping.

To be honest, I relished surprises for the same reason.

When we reached the campsite, the circus folk, seated at a cluster of picnic tables, were eating communal dinner outside their wagons before the evening performance. The air was thick with smoke and the smell of grilled food. Nellie was at the serving station, scooping roast chicken from a cast-iron pot onto a tin plate for Ringmaster Clyde. Clyde had removed his jacket and was sporting an undershirt and muscular arms. I tipped my hat to them both.

"Miss Nellie Brown," I said. "My name is Crimson, and I'm here to make you an offer."

Staring at me dead-on, unimpressed and unblinking, she mechanically reached for another plate. She dished chicken and potatoes, and handed me a wooden spoon.

"Thank you, Miss Nellie," I said, accepting the food, which was piping hot. "I'm leaving for Utah. If you're willing, you could be of value to me in scouting Goblin Valley at the behest of President Lincoln."

She didn't say anything, her blank gaze steady, but she didn't stop me from talking.

"Job pays a hundred dollars, and you don't have to cook or clean. We'll leave that to Bad Jace, though, honestly, I'd prefer anyone else to prepare a meal." I blew on the chicken to cool it before tasting. "You know, this is excellent grub."

Ringmaster Clyde wasn't happy. He lay his untouched plate on a table, squeezing both fists to pop his knuckles dramatically. "Boy," he said. "Nellie already has steady work. She's not running off with a scrawny kid cracked enough to believe he works for the Union."

Nellie smiled ever so lightly at Clyde's remark, tilting her head as she examined me more closely. I could see that she was considering my offer.

"Bad Jace," she said. "He the big guy that arrived late to the matinee show?"

"The same," I said. "He doesn't smell good, but he is superb company in hostile territory."

"You saw me doing my knives," she said. "That's why you need me."

I nodded. "Your skills are breathtaking and worthy of a career in law enforcement. Oh, I brought you a present." I handed her one of the Scottish dirks.

She looked at it, moved it around in her hand. "Now *this*," she said. "This is excellent. I like this gift. What's your name again?"

"Crimson."

She started to remove the apron she'd been wearing. "One-hundred and twenty-five dollars, Boy Crimson. I'm ready to go with you. Fools here don't appreciate my cooking."

Ringmaster Clyde said, "Nellie, he's a loon. I won't let you go!" He went to grab her, but she raised the dirk, pointing it at his chest.

I sensed circus folk gathering behind me, making it difficult to leave with Nellie.

"Let her go," I said. I heard the rage in my voice, realizing in an instant that I was no longer speaking to Clyde but to my diabolical father.

Clyde came at me with fury, but I threw my plate of hot chicken into his eyes and sidestepped, tripping him with my boot. His head smashed against the table's edge, eliciting gasps.

Then I heard the whip crack, felt leather braids coil around my neck, choking me. I tried and failed to get my fingers beneath the thong to tear myself loose. The memory of the whip hurt more than the pain it inflicted. Once again though, I fell to my knees, just as I did on my father's plantation, helpless in front of a black woman.

Nellie, however, brandished the blade I'd given her. She used it to slash the whip, releasing me.

She helped me to my feet and gazed defiantly at the circus performers. The lion tamer glared at us, still gripping the handle of his severed whip. The acrobats tended to Clyde, who lay before us groaning. The fat man pinched another piece of chicken from Nellie's pot.

"No offense, y'all, but I need a change. Boy Crimson is offering me a chance to make something of myself. He's also," she said, swatting my backside with a wry grin, "very easy on the eyes."

"Kid," I said hoarsely, rubbing my throat. "Kid Crimson."

NELLIE DONNED HER COWGIRL GARB—OPEN crown hat, plaid shirt, cowskin waistcoat, white woolie chinks on blue denim chaps—and left everything behind except for her money. When Bad Jace saw her approaching, he guffawed appreciatively. He said to Nellie he was happy to tour Utah with a lethal gal. They shook hands firmly before Bad Jace offered to give her a boost into the buckboard. She accepted, then noticed what he'd set up inside the covered wagon.

"Kid," she said, sensing danger yet still intrigued. "Sure this is a law enforcement job? Whatever's in this wagon is sinister."

"Everything we do is authorized by the US government," I lied.

"And anything that's *not* authorized," Bad Jace said, "is done to preserve the Union."

The last part didn't impress Nellie. She got into the driver's seat by step-scaling the giant wheel from one of the spokes to the rim. Grabbing hold of the long brake, she pulled herself up into the buckboard. "I don't care about no Union. I want to tear things apart and never put them back."

Bad Jace and I shared a look of agreement. We hadn't heard our own personal motivations articulated in such precise fashion.

We started down Mount Davidson, the horses straining back in the traces to keep from plunging too fast down the steep grade. Because I didn't have the reins, I had nothing to hold on to except the thin rod around the seat, which made the ride terrifying but exhilarating. Once off the hill and on the trail proper, we jangled merrily across the valley and on our way to Utah.

Nellie pushed our horses a tad too hard, but Bad Jace and I were grateful. We were on what the Mormons called the Loneliest Trail and headed to Goblin Valley before the sun had even begun to descend. Washoe zephyrs reached us, blasting us with hot wind as we shielded our eyes with our hands. Our horses had enjoyed plenty of rest and were strong against relentless grit. We no longer saw the tracks of Colonel Connor's regiment but expected to pick them up again later.

Eventually darkness fell. Night riding was my favorite way to travel during Nevada summers, especially when I had good company and heavy firepower in tow. Nellie seemed to be born for road work, swigging mightily from a canteen of cold coffee that Bad Jace had prepared for the trip, brewed strong enough to float a horseshoe. The wind was loud, but she regaled us in her husky Southern twang with a story of how she'd gotten her start in entertainment as an alligator wrestler in St. Augustine, Florida. The alligator farm there had been a tourist attraction in the years before the war, but a deep freeze had damaged the citrus industry, which impacted the entire state economy. The owner of the farm couldn't afford to feed the gators regularly, and Nellie found herself trying to pin the jaws of desperately hungry reptiles no smaller than six feet in length. She'd nearly lost a leg when a mammoth gator chomped her.

"God didn't put me on this earth to be eaten by a lizard," she said.

"There are gators in Georgia," I said. "I didn't wrestle them. My father organized boat tours along the Apalachicola. We shot hundreds of gators for the entertainment of financiers."

Nellie offered no comment.

"The more I hear about your father," Bad Jace said, "the more I like him."

"You'd envy his evil. Makes you seem like a choirboy."

"Ha! Kid, I *was* a choirboy. Until I turned eleven and got booted out for indecency."

"Tried to set the church ablaze, Bad Jace?"

"Nah, I grew too fond of the old-maid organist. She was a pretty bird."

"Wow, how old was she?"

"Fifty-two."

"Well, you were an ambitious chorister."

"Still am. I can sing the hell out of a hymn."

"You should team up with Chaparral on a song."

"You know, he punches hard for a musician. I respect that."

"What about you, Nellie? Any musical ability?"

Nellie remained silent. Then she stopped the carriage and pulled the lantern off the wagon hook to illuminate our faces. "Kid, I think I know who your daddy is. If I'm right, it makes sense that you're here, two thousand miles away from his plantation."

Her words froze me to the buckboard. I wanted to ask her what she knew of my father, but a rifle cracked in the distance.

We stayed quiet, listening in the darkness until we heard another shot.

"That's close," Bad Jace said.

"Ain't no gunfight," Nellie insisted. "Same rifle."

"Hunting maybe," I said.

A woman screamed.

Bad Jace and I didn't have to say anything. Nellie slapped the reins, and we were off.

6

We pushed the wagon for a hundred yards before Nellie quietly brought the horses to a halt behind a bluff to scout out the situation. On the other side of the hill, the woman yelped, indicating that she was threatened. The gunfire had ceased.

Bad Jace grabbed a rifle, Nellie unsheathed her knives, and I drew my Colt. We slinked up and along the bare, rocky outcroppings, careful not to kick any loose rocks. When we reached the summit, the problem was more desperate than I'd imagined.

A blonde woman held, from the wrong end, a Winchester, which had jammed or run out of bullets. The moon, full and bright, illuminated her as she clumsily swung the stock of her rifle at three men, who'd obviously crept up to her campsite and tried to assault her, her horse blowing and snorting in alarm. Her effort to defend herself was pathetic, as she wore a travel dress with black lace and cream fichu trimmings, fitted bodice, and a bustle overskirt. She lost her balance mid-swing and tumbled into the grass, nearly falling into the flickering fire she'd arranged within a cluster of cottonwoods along a meandering stream.

The derby-wearing man pounced, wrenching the rifle from her grip. As she regained her balance, she turned to run, but he grabbed her skirt and yanked her off her feet. Her face slammed into the ground, which elicited a laugh from the goons. They stood over her groaning form now, chuckling darkly and unfastening their belts.

Bad Jace raised his Winchester, but I grabbed the barrel. "You might hit her," I hissed. "Nellie, shall we leave this to you?"

She nodded, then sprang into action, blades concealed.

She scampered down the craggy hill, pebbles clacking. The bushwhackers heard the noise and spread themselves apart to avoid getting shot in a cluster. They drew their guns on whatever was coming at them. Nellie stepped into the firelight, hands raised to show she was unarmed.

She said, feigning skittishness, "Can you spare something to eat, gentlemen? Heard a shot and figured y'all hunting. I'm awful hungry."

"We sure can," the tallest one said, grinning. "Come here, girl, and we'll feed you."

The bushwhackers laughed, holstering their guns except for the one that spoke first.

"Looks like we got white meat," said another one, "*and* dark meat tonight, fellas!"

More laughter. Bad Jace again raised the barrel and in the moonlight, I could see his clenched jaw and quivering trigger finger.

Suspicious, the tallest bushwhacker said, "You alone, girl? Anyone out there with you?"

"By myself." She sighed with exasperation. "Horse done run off. Had all my food in the saddle."

"Well, now," he said, lowering his gun arm. "We're happy to give you food. First, though, you'll need to do me a little favor."

Bad Jace and I couldn't see Nellie's face, but we observed her slowly approach the bushwhacker and give him her hand. The others made their way to the unconscious woman, the one wearing horn-rimmed glasses reaching down to grab her long blonde hair to pull her face up from the dirt.

"Pretty," he said with a sick giggle.

From the sound of his grinding teeth, I could tell my partner was good and ready to get on with the killing, even if it meant all five of them. "What the hell is Nellie doing, Kid?" he said, voice rising. "She can't fight."

I shushed him. "She can definitely fight. She's a human mantis."

"A *what* now?"

"Be a good girl for me," the bushwhacker said to her.

"I'll be so good," Nellie cooed, letting him touch her face.

The bushwhacker went to kiss her in the darkness. There was the sound of cutting meat and a shout of agony.

"Seth?" said his buddy. "What the hell's—"

Seth collapsed to the ground, his sliced-open guts spilling out into a pool beside his dead body.

The others heard the wet splatter, stunned by the horror.

"Jesus!" said Spectacles, getting off a futile shot.

Nellie threw the first knife directly into his throat. He gurgled his own blood, falling backward as his second shot blew the derby off his buddy's head.

The Guns of Goblin Valley

"I'm killed!" the derbyless last man standing screamed into the darkness.

"You ain't," she said, spin-tossing the Scottish dirk high into the air. "But now you are."

As the blade came down, she reached up, caught it by the tip, and sent it flying into the man's eye socket.

He fell to his knees, trying to yank the knife free. The life gradually faded from his body, and he keeled over dead.

Bad Jace stared at the scene, mouth open in astonishment. "Kid, have you—"

"Never seen anything like it. But I told you what she was capable of, ye of little faith..."

We scampered down from the bluff and surveyed the carnage. Bad Jace and I palmed the top of our hats as we stepped around the gore, struggling to process it all. Nellie had already propped the woman up against the trunk of a cottonwood, dabbing the cuts on her face with a cloth damp with creek water.

"You two throw wood on that fire before it goes out," Nellie said. "And then grab a skillet and some of that bacon and beans that I brought in the wagon. Killing fools gets me hungry enough to eat the north end of a southbound goat."

"Lady gonna make it?" Bad Jace said.

"They licked the red off her candy," she said, "but she'll be fine."

Our hunger ruined by Nellie's savage antics, Bad Jace and I moved the wagon and horses to the woman's camp. I cooked Nellie her pig meat while Bad Jace dragged the bodies away from the fire and into the part of the bluff where the gravel was loose. I grabbed one of the shovels from the wagon, placed there by Grover who foresaw the need, between Bad Jace and me, for burials. I dug a hole, into which I scoop-pushed the entrails. I'd seen plenty of death working with Grover in his funeral parlor, but what Nellie did to these men was worse than a Comanche attack.

While our knife-happy assassin filled her steel stomach, I helped Bad Jace pile rocks on top of the dead.

"I don't think I'll eat tonight," Bad Jace said.

"Me neither."

"Know what's really scary?"

"Tell me."

"She didn't get a drop of their blood on her. Even as she carved up the one called Seth."

"It is," I said, "a bit uncanny."

When we were done covering the corpses, we rinsed off downstream as the creatures of the night emerged from their hideaways. A coyote yipped in the distance. An owl hooted from its tree perch, then launched into the air, wings flapping. In the creek itself, frogs and insects chorused a symphony of chirps and croaks, tiny voices urging us to wash up and get moving.

When we returned, the unknown woman had regained consciousness. Sitting close to the fire, Nellie was talking to her about voodoo rituals in Louisiana. The woman had a bowl of beans in her lap and looked much better and prettier now that she was no longer splayed on the ground.

"Hello, boys," Nellie said, sitting cross-legged next to the woman. "Let me introduce you to Miss Lydia Sweet, a certified educator from Oregon."

Bad Jace removed his hat, long hair spilling to his shoulders, and introduced himself. Me, I didn't go in for useless chivalry, but I went ahead and nodded, pinched my brim, and said, "I'm Kid Crimson. What *kind* of educator are you, Miss Sweet?"

"I'm a teacher of children," she said, voice shaking from her recent trauma. "I'm on my way to the mining town of Virginia City, where I hope to provide the kind of moral and intellectual instruction that transforms the frontier chaos of children's lives into a civilized oasis." Her hands trembled. "I—I must sound a bit loopy to you right now."

She did sound strange, as if she'd just recited a speech she'd been practicing.

It seemed Bad Jace thought so too. "She hit her head really hard, seems like."

Lydia thought he was referring to her appearance and pulled a compact from her purse. Then she realized that Bad Jace was chiding her plan to improve Virginia City. "What I meant to say is…uh, I mean…oh, I don't know what I mean. Something about a proper foundation in mathematics and a passing knowledge of the writings of William Shakespeare."

"Who needs Shakespeare," I said, "when you have the scribblings of Samuel Clemens printed daily in your hometown?"

Bad Jace guffawed. "Clemens can write an entertaining yarn. He's no bard though."

"I know the name," Lydia said, taking a small bite of beans. "I believe he's a reporter for the *Territorial Enterprise*. He wrote the article that inspired me to seek out Virginia City."

"Which article?" I said. I squatted by the fire, blinking the sleep from my eyes while pouring a cup of the coffee that Nellie had cooked.

"The one that stated there is to be an examination of candidates for positions as teachers in the new public school in Virginia City."

I'd read the column, thinking it meant the end of Ezra

and Sarah's innocence. I'd despised my own schooling in Georgia, where teachers drilled the Bible and the National Poet of England into the children's brains. "If you're from Oregon," I said, "you're coming from the wrong direction."

"I was visiting my sister in Durango," Lydia said. "Another prospector's paradise."

"Why not teach there?"

"The elevation—nine thousand feet in the air—doesn't agree with me. I suffer at high altitudes."

"You might suffer in Virginia City," Bad Jace said. "The altitude there is six thousand feet."

"You nearly suffered here in the floodplain," I pointed out. "Lucky for you, Nellie was ready."

"Yes, I was just thanking her for her help. I could've used her intervention earlier today when I encountered the soldiers."

Bad Jace grunted, sat down cross-legged by the fire. "Soldiers in Union blue?"

Lydia nodded. "They stole my food, and they would've taken more if Colonel Connor hadn't scolded the evil troll."

"Evil troll?" I said.

"You-ship. You-seff. Both his eyes were blackened."

"Ustick," Bad Jace said. "Kid, you tussled with him back in Virginia City."

"I did. Clearly, I didn't hit him hard enough."

"He had fresh scalps, too," she continued, "hanging from his belt."

"We didn't encounter any Paiutes on the trail. Do you know where they got them?"

"They mentioned something about a prison transport."

Bad Jace shook his head, confused. "Had to be a federal transport. Why did Connor intercept it?"

"Who knows," I said. "Maybe the Paiutes escaped the transport, and Connor pursued."

Lydia yawned. "Forgive me, but I've suddenly grown tired."

"Rest," Nellie said, applying a warm cloth to the teacher's forehead, the angel of death now serving as an angel of mercy. "One of us will escort you to Virginia City."

"I saw the mule cart that belonged to the bushwhackers," Bad Jace said. "I'll water and feed the animals now, and in the morning, I'll accompany you to town, Miss Sweet."

I gave him a look and was about to say something, then thought better of it.

Nellie noticed my calculation and smiled. "Looks like you and I, Kid, are following Connor to Goblin Valley."

"If that's indeed where he's going," I said. "So far, he appears to be fulfilling his stated purpose of killing Indians."

"Why kill the native people," Lydia said, "when there are so many bandits plaguing the area?"

"I think we all know the answer to your question."

"Kid," Bad Jace said. "I'll catch up with you and Miss Nellie as soon as I get Miss Sweet to the teacher examination."

"I hate to be a burden to you all," she said. "It seems you've embarked on an important mission, and I've gummed it up."

"Not at all," I said. "You've given us some valuable information."

"I hope to meet this Ustick gentleman tomorrow,"

Nellie said, producing a blade and balancing the point of it on her finger.

I noticed Lydia swallow anxiously with the realization that Nellie had a vicious side. Then the schoolhouse woman passed her bowl to Bad Jace, who initially waved it away, then capitulated it and began spooning beans into his ravenous maw.

"Let me apologize in advance," he said while chewing, "if this meal causes me to trumpet."

Lydia covered her mouth to giggle and swatted her new bodyguard.

7

I DIDN'T LIKE THE IDEA OF TRACKING COLONEL Connor to Goblin Valley without Bad Jace, but it couldn't be helped. Leaving Lydia alone on the trail would have been a dumber move than she'd made herself by being there alone, and I certainly wasn't the one to accompany a homework hag—comely as she might be—back to Virginia City. It might undermine my reputation in town and drive a wedge between Ezra and me. If the boy loathed anything, it was sitting still at a schoolhouse desk. Also, I had to consider the sardonic pen of Clemens, his talents becoming less useful to me as word spread about my exploits in a mining town at the edge of the world. Clemens and I were chums. But I knew he couldn't resist writing an article that savored the irony of a deadly gun escorting a fair-haired symbol of civilized values into a city of greed and violence. Better for Bad Jace to occupy that role, for better or worse for him, leaving Nellie and me to investigate a Mormon steelworks operation in remote, desolate terrain, full of narrow canyons winding through sandstone cliffs.

Having observed Nellie carving up bandits gave me pause. I'd anticipated bringing along a dangerous companion, but what I witnessed was unfathomable. All night I tossed and turned in my blanket, unable to sleep as I imagined having to square off in a knife fight against utter remorseless lethality. I was no slouch when it came to bladed weapons—hell, with my Bowie, I could pin a butterfly to the skirt of a donkey's saddle from several yards. But Nellie had transformed into a wildcard, an unpredictable force that I had to direct toward the enemy —whoever that ended up being.

Maybe I had nothing to worry about, and Nellie would do her job and do it well.

Or maybe she'd kill everyone around her, just to work up an appetite. If I had her ability to toss knives with fatal accuracy, I might've done so for the sheer hell of it.

I got a few hours of sleep before dawn. Being the first one to wake, I stirred Nellie. Her eyes popped open, and we suited up in the dark. I stoked the embers, put on coffee for us, and heated up beans and bacon in case anyone was hungry. It turned out Lydia had a black buggy with a Belgian Draught that Bad Jace was already feeding with a blend of hay and nearby grass. I brought him a copper mug and observed him repair Lydia's rifle, boot propped on a mossy boulder. Using her nail file, he carefully lifted the extractor off the rim of the live round, then pushed the carrier down with the round still in it. Then he extracted the spent round with the file, making the gun functional.

"Good work," I said, handing him a steaming mug. "Now your new girlfriend can shoot any bandits chasing you to Virginia City."

He smiled. "She's unlike any woman I've met. She reads Latin."

"Dead language."

"Well, you would know."

"Know what?"

"The language of the deceased." He didn't smile when he said it. "You can handle Nellie?"

I wasn't going to admit to a possible miscalculation. "Of course. Tell Poppy that I—" Words failed me in the moment.

"I'll let her know you miss her," Bad Jace said, saving me. "Kid, look, I can't be the only one giving you this advice. Marry that girl before someone else does—someone with stronger moral fiber and a bigger pocketbook."

"I'm trying my best. Men like us have to work harder to land a bride."

Bad Jace chuckled. "You mean, to find a woman whose face doesn't scare a vulture off a gut pile."

Lydia began walking up, smiling and beautiful even after she'd obviously spent a night like I did. She yawned and stretched like a towheaded dream. Bad Jace handed her his coffee. "Ready, Miss Sweet?"

Her smile faded with a sigh. "I suppose so," she said, looking tired and sounding forlorn.

"Crimson," Nellie said, sleek and pretty in her own right. "Let's get moving. You drive first."

"Sounds good. All right, Miss Sweet, see you in town. Bad Jace, with any luck, I'll see *you* in a few days."

He nodded, giving Nellie a side glance. "I'll send a telegram in case you stop in Silver Reef."

I gave him a wink. "We'd love to hear from you."

Nellie and I hopped into the buckboard, heading in the direction of Goblin Valley, wondered when and if we'd catch up with Colonel Connor and when and if Bad Jace would catch up with us. The morning light cast the red sandstone formations with an otherworldly aura as we watched a bighorn sheep scramble down a steep cliff, surefooted and agile.

Lydia's detail about the scalps troubled me, making me question my decision to blacken Ustick's eyes instead of breaking his arms. It was yet another indication that, at my advanced age of twenty-four years, I was starting to mellow. Maybe it was due to living in Virginia City, a town increasingly infested with soft-handed bankers and lawyers who recently seemed to outnumber the hardscrabble miners. Maybe it was being with Poppy, the town opium nymph and the loveliest creature who ever roamed the earth. In any case, if I had the chance, I planned to finish what I'd started with Ustick, making it impossible for him to hurt anyone ever again. I was still livid about him smacking Ezra and Sarah and injuring my friend Chaparral, the piano player. Violence was in my blood, and the more I struggled to push this aspect of myself away, the more agitated I became. So much for my mellowing. My rage required a release valve; the monster inside needed to be unleashed from time to time.

Otherwise, everyone would suffer, in Virginia City and beyond.

"Yesterday," I said to Nellie, "you suggested that you knew my father."

She looked at me for a long moment, then settled her gaze on the trail in front of us. "Alligator shooting," she said, "isn't common in Georgia. There's only one man, a slave-owner, who puts them on. I imagine he's your father, and I hear he's a royal bastard."

I didn't take offense. My father was worse than a bastard. "What else did you hear?"

"That he had a son he nearly killed with his own hands. A boy who left when the war began."

"I knew you were from the South. Your accent is Louisiana, not Georgia."

"Still, word gets around. I wasn't no slave though. My daddy white."

"Same here."

"Well, mine died from yellow fever. He was a doctor, a surgeon."

"He the one who taught you to use knives?"

"Nah, I learned how to blade from Marie Laveau."

"The voodoo queen of New Orleans."

She nodded. "She taught me knives and necromancy."

"Well, I hope she taught you to shoot."

"My mama taught me how to use a gun. You require ballistics?"

"Urgently," I said, indicating the dust cloud ahead, kicked up by a fast-moving wagon.

"Who that?"

"Whiskey trader. You can tell by the barrels."

"Well, they won't have anything left to trade by going *that* fast."

"Paiutes chasing."

Rifles cracked in the distance, our horses emitting sharp, panicked whinnies.

"How many?"

"Five."

"Why should we help whiskey traders?"

"Because," I said, "I'm pretty sure Verbena is the intended recipient of all that liquor."

"She runs the Blood Nugget."

"Indeed."

Nellie smirked, loading the Henry repeating rifle that I'd given her with .44 caliber cartridges. "How many rounds this take?"

"You're scaring me." I wasn't *really* scared. I was excited by the oncoming butchery.

"Wait until you see me shoot."

IT DIDN'T TAKE LONG. I whipped the reins against our horses, increasing our speed toward the whiskey wagon charging right at us, all four horses in a lather.

"What, gonna run them off the trail, Crimson?" Nellie yelled over the din.

I said nothing, drawing my Colt and leveling it at the wagon. Its wheels struck a rock, causing a barrel to fall off the back and roll into the desert scrub.

Nellie raised her rifle, unsure where to aim. We heard the Paiutes yelling and the sound of gunfire, but we didn't spot any warriors.

"We'll come up the wagon's left side," I shouted. "Shoot whoever's coming up behind them."

The wagon came into view, the driver's face terror-stricken as he snapped the leather straps, horses at a full gallop. He raised one hand in the air, signaling us to stop and go back.

We were past the point of return.

Our horses and the beasts of the onrushing wagon nearly collided, metal buckles and loops of the harnesses clanging on impact, the lantern next to Nellie's head smashed by the other carriage.

To her credit, she didn't flinch.

Without much distance between us and the Paiute, Nellie and I squeezed off a few shots, hitting nothing. But we succeeded in slowing down the attackers and drawing them to us. I yanked hard on the reins, bringing the horses to a stop.

"Hell you doing?" Nellie said through gritted teeth.

I jumped into the wagon bonnet and used my Bowie to slash the wooden bows, fabric collapsing all around me to reveal the Gatling gun that Bad Jace had mounted to the bed and sideboards. A thing of ominous beauty, the gun comprised ten barrels revolving around a central axis. A top-mounted magazine holding a hundred rounds fed the gun, fired by rotating the barrels with a hand crank. I stood behind it and, knowing it was loaded, started cranking.

Nellie gasped. "Crimson crazy as an outhouse rat!"

The Paiutes had whipped around to come at us. Before they could bring their horses to a canter, I blasted two of them off their saddles. The clangor of death was spine-tingling.

I wasn't used to such tremendous firepower, however. I wasted too many rounds before realizing that the machine's crosshairs were worthless and I was blasting any stray hot-air balloons out of the sky. The remaining Paiute galloped away, heading toward the sandstone formations of Buckskin Gulch.

"Woo-hoo!" Nellie yelled, standing on the buckboard with her rifle in the air. "Crimson, that was more fun than the circus!"

Registering that the gunfire had ceased, the whiskey trader slowed and turned around to wave. I jumped off our wagon to beckon him.

"Nellie," I said. "Would you please fetch the whiskey barrel he dropped?"

"Yessir," she said, sitting down again to grab the reins.

As she wheeled down the trail, I scanned Buckskin Gulch to confirm no one was circling back. The whiskey trader seemed apprehensive, looking in the same direction too, as he drew closer with his wagon, a rifle balanced in the crook of his arm.

"Hello," I said. "Name's Crimson. You bringing that whiskey to Virginia City?"

"You're a shrewd young fellow," he said, reaching from the driver's seat to shake my hand. "Jellicoe."

"I heard the Blood Nugget was expecting a shipment this week. But not by stage."

Jellicoe scoffed. "Well, I hoped to make a little money on the way there."

I walked around to inspect the bed of his wagon, laden with barrels and glass pint containers with metal lids, and a significant pile of buffalo robes.

"You've been trading with the Ute."

He started to turn toward me but seemed anxious about it. Still in his seat, Jellicoe said, "Yep. Got some nice furs out of the deal I hope to sell in California."

I had a suspicion. Grabbed an empty glass pint, and unscrewed the lid. Then I took out my Bowie to punch a hole in one of the barrels. Liquor gushed out in a stream, which I caught in the container.

"Weak. You mixed it with…tea, I suspect."

"Yep, goes further."

I tried another taste. "It's bad. Verbena won't like this at all."

"Well, I, uh," he stammered, stepping down from the buckboard to address my concerns. "I don't intend to bring any of that to Virginia City!"

"You got the real whiskey back here somewhere?"

"Yes, in those barrels."

I punched a hole in one and drew a taste. Worse.

"Jellicoe," I said, the monster stirring in its chains. "Verbena is a good friend of mine."

"Now, Crimson, you punched a hole in the wrong

barrel. I got the good whiskey marked on the bottom, see. But I know my business, and I need you to stop taste-testing every damned thing."

Someone coughed beneath the buffalo robes.

I yanked away the furs to find a girl, younger looking and smaller than Sarah, blonde and dirty-faced, looking at me. Her dress was covered in blood and looked burned in places. Her expression told me things.

The chains fell away, the monster famished.

I drew my Colt and pointed it at Jellicoe. He'd left his rifle in the driver's seat and wasn't carrying a pistol. "Explain."

"She—well, she…" he said, trembling. "I picked her up near the site of an Indian massacre. A group of Paiute killed a small caravan of settlers a few miles back, so I took her in. Fed her. Grilled some bison steaks and gave her water, lots of it. Coffee too. She hid 'neath them furs when Paiute attacked us is why she's there."

"I think there's another reason she's hiding." I aimed at his leg.

By this time, Nellie had returned with the barrel that had fallen from Jellicoe's wagon. "Crimson, what's the scenario here?"

I was about to pull the trigger when the girl screamed and jumped from the wagon with my Bowie that I'd left beside the watered-down whiskey barrel.

She managed to jab the knife just below Jellicoe's collarbone, holding onto the handle as she fell so the blade bit deeply, ripping apart his subclavian artery. She left the knife in him as she stepped away, breathing heavily. Blood geysered, his white shirt turning red.

"Killed me, you little bitch," Jellicoe groaned, folding in on himself and sinking into the dust.

The monster had nothing to eat at this point. In a

voice that wasn't my own, I told Nellie to bring the girl to our wagon.

"Okay, but what about all this?"

"Go now."

As she led the girl away, I yanked the knife from Jellicoe, gouged holes in all the barrels, and turned over all the pint containers. Then I grabbed a box of matches, struck one, and tossed it into the alcohol, igniting the wagon.

Despite being watered down, the whiskey burned. Jellicoe hadn't lied about carrying barrels of the real stuff to Virginia City after all.

I admired the inferno for some time. When I looked toward Buckskin Gulch, the Paiutes were mounted less than a hundred yards away, staring at the carnage I'd created. I stared back. But I felt rotten about killing two of their brothers to save a, well, dead man. Then again, I felt good about sparing the live ones the agony of alcohol poisoning.

Eventually, they turned their horses toward the sun and trotted away, leaving me in the flames.

8

Nellie and the girl waited for me in the wagon, the hand-cranked gun shrouded in canvas. Sitting in the driver's seat, the girl, wrapped in a blanket, gazed silently at the horizon from which Jellicoe had brought her. It was the same direction of the massacre site, according to the whiskey trader. I took a running leap into the wagon bed and settled in for the ride, my back to the driver's box so that I could confirm the Paiute didn't follow. I'd anticipated questions, but Nellie seemed to realize I wasn't in the mood to explain anything.

Instead, she said, "Her name is Dolly. Dolly Boyer."

Dolly said nothing; didn't turn around for a hello or a handshake. She stayed silent, sullen, as our cart rollicked along the trail. When I looked westward, I saw the sun beginning its descent, blue sky dimming as the haze and dust of the atmosphere turned the clouds blood red.

"We should go a few more miles," I said, "and camp for the night."

"We doing shifts?" Nellie said. "This trail is busier than a cat crap-covering a marble floor."

"I know a place where we can sleep. I have friends, even at the edge of the world."

"I hope your friend has whiskey. I see you decided to burn it all and bring none back."

"He has that and more."

"Think the Paiute will follow?"

"No, they seemed…satisfied."

"With what?"

"With how I handled the problem of a cheating whiskey trader."

"You killed two warriors!"

"They shot first."

"Ha! I've heard *that* before."

"Besides, if they want me, they can come and take me."

"I've also heard that before. Don't worry, Crimson," she said, snatching the hat from my head and plopping it on Dolly's flaxen crown. "My new friend and I won't let them drag you off."

The girl smiled and drew the chin strap tight to keep the wind from blowing the hat away.

I couldn't help but smile too. I didn't want to ask Dolly how badly Jellicoe had hurt her. I'd been wounded enough as a child to know there was no point in asking. All that mattered was helping Dolly put the pieces of her life together. I had the luck of finding a father figure like Grover, and the love of a beautiful woman like Poppy. As long as I stayed close to them, there was a chance I might live to find happiness in a world plagued by men who cherished hurting other men, their own women, and children. Out here, in forsaken places like Nevada and Utah, the law was unfocused, disorganized. Out here, I could devise my own rules and evade a brutal conflict that made no sense to me, that made no sense to any god looking down from the sky. War was a moral campaign waged against those who had no real say in whatever was being fought over. Blood spilled never belonged to perpetrators of evil. The cruel slavers and slave ship firms that caused the horror of slavery would never be punished, while tens of thousands of my young, ignorant, redneck brothers were dying, and not gloriously, on a battlefield of muck and blood, or miserably in a disease-ridden prison camp.

My father had damaged me so badly that I believed in no causes. I revered nothing except accumulating enough wealth to buy a citrus farm in California, with my son in Poppy's belly as we toured the orchards in a fancy buggy pulled by a white horse.

I'd never admit to believing in God. However, if He gave me Poppy, I might privately repent.

But only if He made her mine forever.

My friend in the wasteland was known as the Desert Saint. He wasn't an ordained priest, nor was he Catholic, as far as I knew. Father Ephraim was a religious hermit, having established a place of worship and respite inside a seventy-foot sandstone cave within nearby Graves Valley, Utah. The Ute Indians avoided it, since the cave, according to legend, served as a cursed repository for skinwalkers, where the dead lost their souls to demons, never to be rescued. Father Ephraim took advantage of this belief, using the cave to pray for peace and the return of the Savior.

He also used the cave to hide outlaws, as long as they had money. The grotto was impossible to access by bounty hunters and soldiers, providing no cover as they tried to scamper down a hundred yards or more of sheer sandstone to reach the mouth. Once in the cave, Father Ephraim could access an unknown number of small, crawl-on-your-belly outlets, each arriving at a different part of the vast canyon. To cover every exit required a large posse, one of two things that made it tricky to snare a bandit befriended by the reclusive saint.

The other thing being that Father Ephraim was a crack shot and a born scrapper.

The sun plummeted as we drove in darkness. When we reached the creek that ran near Graves Valley, I unharnessed the horses, bringing them water and whatever grass I could find. Nellie hopped off the wagon and helped Dolly down before getting a fire going. Soon we wolfed down the last bit of bacon and beans, Nellie regaling little Dolly with a tale of the summoning of a prankish spirit during a voodoo ritual in New Orleans. In her story, the *loa* ended up possessing an artist, wife of a prominent politician, who dabbled in witchcraft. The artist sculpted a statue of a Catahoula Leopard Dog, a piece so lifelike that it won an award. When the statue was sold to a collector in Louisiana and displayed in his home, the statue disappeared, only to show up the next day in the artist's workshop. Time and again, the sculpture was placed in a wagon and hauled to the collector's house only to vanish in the night and return to the artist in the morning. This went on for an entire year, until Marie Laveau, voodoo queen of New Orleans, finally dispelled the impish loa from the artist's heart in a spectacularly unnerving ceremony.

"Wait, the statue turned into a dog?" Dolly said, laughing.

"The statue was a totem of dark magic," Nellie said. "Eventually, a *real* leopard dog arrived at the artist's doorstep after the ceremony. The two have been best friends ever since."

"Can't befriend a demon," a voice growled from the darkness beyond our firelight.

Dolly gasped. I leaped to my boots and drew my pistol, though I had no intention to pull the trigger. I recognized the gravelly bass.

In one fell swoop, Nellie drew a blade from a scabbard on her belt and jumped back, placing herself solidly between the man and the little girl.

"Nellie, wait!!"

A robed man with a beard and shock of white hair stepped forward, carrying what looked like the panel of an armored wagon.

Dolly's mouth fell open but didn't make a sound.

"Miss Nellie, Dolly, allow me to introduce," I said, "Father Ephraim, the Desert Saint."

As Father Ephraim led us through the mouth of the cave, the bustling wind and terrestrial hum of the darkness outside was crushed by a deeper darkness. He wielded a lantern to guide us, with each step the sand beneath our boots rustling like grains in an invisible hourglass. The air carried the sharp tang of minerals and guano, a scent at once earthy and unappetizing. Ancient forces sculpted this labyrinth and would continue to carve it long after our bodies turned to dust.

"We've never had women in the monastery," he said, moving around a massive stalagmite that had erupted from the cavern floor like a gloomy sentinel. "Never imagined it was possible. But every day offers new desperation and a fresh horror."

I couldn't see Nellie's face, but I guessed she didn't like what she heard. "We had a run-in with some Paiute," I explained. "Seemed like a good moment to call in a favor, Father."

The favor was unforgettable. My friend Snake and I had arrived here years ago, running from a vengeful posse that blamed us for a deadly saloon shootout that had nothing to do with us. Another gunfighter-and-his-Indian-buddy duo had killed the sheriff, then lit out in our direction. Soon enough, Snake and I were hunted over a crudely rendered wanted poster, causing us to scamper for our lives into Graves Valley. There we found refuge...and a man who, by happenstance, had just been bit by Gila monster. Father Ephraim had tried to burn the venom at the injection site before it could poison his bloodstream, damaging his leg in the process. I applied carbolic acid to his wound, the way I'd read about Union army surgeons doing it in an article I'd read in *The Atlantic*, and it worked. I'd procured some of the stuff to keep me from dying from infection, keeping it in my saddlebag even now. There was only one scenario of annihilation that I'd accept—a hail of lead.

"Anyone who withdraws kindness from a friend," Father Ephraim said as we began squeezing through a narrow passage, "forsakes the fear of the Almighty. It's in the Good Book, Crimson. You and I are friends, and together we fear God and are loved by Him."

"Thank you, Father."

"Tell me about the black woman from New Orleans," he went on. "She's pretty, which I like. She's also dangerous, which I don't like. She drew that knife and was ready to throw even before I'd finished my sentence."

"Right behind you, Father," she said. "My name is Nellie, and I'm happy to tell you—"

Dolly suddenly sneezed, which inspired Ephraim to say, "God bless." Then he said, "Nellie, what do you think of this war the president has conjured? Will your people be set free?"

"I don't know," she said. "Everyone wears chains from where I stand. And all those barefooted, lice-ridden, blonde boys in Confederate Gray look shackled to Death himself."

Father Ephraim stopped in his tracks and turned to face Nellie, bringing the lantern toward her features. "If I had not sworn off earthly pleasures, I'd marry you, Bayou Girl." Then he continued moving through the gloom.

I stood behind her, so Nellie turned and whispered, "Does he know he's old and ugly?"

Just when I thought we could go no further, we emerged into a vast chamber bathed in soft firelight. The walls curved away into the distance, surfaces shimmering with iridescent hues as if painted by the hand of a prehistoric wizard. I could tell that Nellie and Dolly were in a state of awe and wonder, seeing the hidden beauty that simmered beneath the crust of the earth. The sound of the chamber was like a liquid dream, aqueous and eternal, a lullaby for the haunted brain. A salve for the lacerated mind.

Strangely enough, Father Ephraim had three blankets and pillows ready for us. Glass bottles of water, too. Even a teddy bear for Dolly. Did he see us coming from miles away?

"Father," I said. "Were you expecting us?"

"Last night, I dreamed of your imminent arrival. There are sinister forces at work here in Utah. Sleep will help you gather your powers."

"What kind of forces?" Nellie said.

"There's a regiment of Union soldiers tearing across

the desert. They seek something that they believe will turn the tide of war against them."

"Father, you must know about the Mormons and their munitions factory," I said, dropping the saddle I'd been carrying next to a blanket. "Is it true they're building arms for the South?"

"For the South? More likely that any arms fashioned will be directed at mining towns."

"Mining towns? What for?"

"For the silver and the gold. For treasure."

"Come on, Father. The South can't use precious metals to defeat Lincoln. That stuff has to be converted into weapons."

"Have you wondered," he said, "about who benefits from war? From the manufacture and sale of munitions, Mr. Crimson?"

"The war merchants, obviously. But why risk the war coming to a halt simply to take over a bunch of risky prospecting pits?"

"Because, Crimson, those prospecting pits finance Lincoln's efforts to obliterate the South."

"Wait, you're saying—"

"Oh, he said it, Crimson Boy," Nellie interrupted. "Someone's bringing the big guns into the Western quarries to take all the metals. Including Virginia City, where your China Girl lives."

I didn't know how to respond to this. The thought was too horrifying to contemplate.

"I'll wake you," Father Ephraim said. "There's cornbread and butter for breakfast."

"Butter?" Nellie said. "You make butter in a canyon?"

"Not me. The Mormon wives, of whom there seem to be many."

"Where are these Mormons?" I asked.

"You'll meet them. First, rest."

Like a shadow, Father Ephraim glided across the canyon walls and was gone before I could figure which passage he took.

Dolly had curled up in her blanket, teddy bear embraced, thumb in her mouth. Eyes closed, she appeared to have drifted right to sleep.

Nellie removed her boots, splayed an array of knives beside her blanket, and tucked in. Soon she was asleep.

The fire beside our blankets crackled, the coziness enticing, even as my head spun at the idea of Virginia City being invaded by Johnny Reb, Mormons, the Knights of the Golden Circle.

This was turning out to be more than a scouting mission. If I located this munitions factory, I'd have no choice but to destroy it before a single cannon could be forged and pointed at Ezra, Sarah, and Poppy.

9

FATHER EPHRAIM RETURNED TO STAND OVER ME and nudge me awake with his sandaled toes. Another night of little sleep, and as I sat up and reached out for the coffee he was handing me, I noticed sunlight filtering through crevices above us.

"Thanks, Father," I said, taking a sip. There was whiskey in it. Good whiskey.

"Get your friends ready," he said, placing a chipped ceramic plate of warm cornbread and soft butter on the ground next to me. "I have someone who will take you to the steelworks."

I immediately stood up. "That was fast."

"You won't like him." Since it was now possible to see quite easily in the cave, Father Ephraim picked up a flat rock, scooped dirt, and tossed it on the embers. "His name is Rocker."

"Rocker Portwell? Father, your social circle has expanded…and grown more virulent."

Rocker was the chief enforcer of the Mormon church, a man as lethal as he was devout. It was rumored that twenty years ago, he'd tried to assassinate the governor of Missouri with a buckshot-loaded Springfield for ordering the expulsion of the Latter-day Saints from his state. I didn't believe the rumor, mainly because the politician lived. My buddy Snake had seen, with his own eyes, Rocker use a rifle to snuff three men from a distance. He was born to kill, enjoyed it.

"Sometimes, in the wilderness, wolves surround us," Father Ephraim said. "But it's in the wilderness that God always finds us."

"Father, I'm only telling you this, because I trust you. I was ordered to spy on the factory, not waltz right into it with a Mormon killer holding the door open."

"Better this way, Kid. Besides, he's interested in you."

"Why is that?"

"Your reputation precedes."

Did Rocker read dime novels? "Well, I look forward to the steelworks tour."

"He does too."

Nellie was stirring at this point. When I offered my coffee, she groggily demurred, grabbed a piece of cornbread, and scarfed. "Mmm. I haven't had cornbread in years. It's not mama's, but pretty good."

"Good morning, Nellie," Father Ephraim said, pouring a hot coffee from a gooseneck pot.

"Morning, Father. Thanks for breakfast. Do you imagine our wagon and horses are still there?"

"I moved them to a different part of the canyon where no one will find them."

Dolly was up now, stretching like a kitten. She stood, blinked, and looked around. "I want to leave this place!"

"Put on your shoes," I said, "and we can go."

"I— I don't have shoes," she said.

Embarrassed by my error, I couldn't bring myself to reply.

The Desert Saint saved me. "I brought towels and soap so the women can bathe. And I have sandals that fit you, Dolly, if you give me a moment," he said, disappearing again into a passage.

"I overheard," Nellie whispered to me. "If Rocker Portwell finds out you're a spy—"

"Technically, I'm not," I said. "I'm working for a Virginia City banker."

"Well, who does the banker work for?"

"I'm...not entirely sure."

Nellie's attention drifted. "Hear that sound?"

"It's a waterfall. Through there," I said, pointing toward a sandstone ingress, "you'll find a hidden lagoon."

"I could use a wash. I'll bring her with me." Then she addressed Dolly. "Little mama?"

The blonde girl stopped chasing a lizard and looked up at her. "Bath time?"

"Yes. Let's go, honey."

Nellie picked up the towels Father Ephraim had brought us, and Dolly took her hand, the two of them walking toward the sound of rushing water.

I drank my coffee, then Nellie's, before eating another piece of cornbread slathered in butter. She'd left her knives behind, and I picked them up, examining each one. The Scottish dirk I'd given her felt sharp to the touch. The other knives were a mix of cutlery, mostly copper-riveted leather handles with heavy steel blades. But I noticed another knife with a symbol etched in the handle—the seal of the Knights of the Golden Circle, a cross with a star in the center.

Miss Nellie, where'd you land such a blade?

I made sure to put everything back where I'd found it. Instead of bathing myself, I cleaned my Colt, blowing out the grit, oiling it, making sure the chamber spun and the sights weren't dented. I took the double bandolier from my saddle to ensure there was a bullet in every ammunition pocket. I slung the black leather belts like a sash over my chest and shoulder in what I called the "Pancho Villa" style, after the Mexican revolutionary general. I rarely wore a bandolier, but if I was going to meet the Mormon church's body count leader, I needed to look imposing.

I remembered something about the "monastery" as Father Ephraim called it, this labyrinthine refuge for wanted men, for those who picked up a gun and threw away the sun. Relying on a lantern the old man had left behind, as well as a vague memory, I navigated into a familiar passageway with a distinctive rock slab—shaped like a beaver—poised diagonally across the mouth of another, eerier series of caves. I slipped through the semi-blocked passage and, following the lantern light, reached a glittering trove of Mexican gold coins, clearly stolen from a train or bank wagon. The gold had been poured messily onto the cave floor, at least ankle deep, with gold bullion and bars in wooden crates available too. Father Ephraim always liked newfangled things, despite resisting new technologies like, well, newspapers and telegrams. He'd long accepted gold from the bandits who lodged in his monastery, but this was clearly a pile brought about by the greed of others—or perhaps by the desire of someone seeking to conquer a mining town like Virginia City.

With *this* kind of money, you could build and finance all types of guns. Was this the stolen gold Ralston had mentioned, bullion to finance Union victory against the

Confederates? I made a mental note about how to find this cavern again and headed back to the campsite.

Nellie and Dolly returned. So did Father Ephraim with a pair of children's sandals, which ended up fitting the girl perfectly.

"You just happen to have girl's shoes?" Nellie said, after donning her clothes behind a boulder.

I held my breath, waiting for his response.

"My daughter," Father Ephraim said, "was exactly Dolly's age when she died."

"Oh. Sorry, Father."

"I'll lead you to Rocker's wagon," Father Ephraim said, ignoring her apology.

Nellie took a breath, and we exchanged looks. I shrugged, biting my tongue to keep from asking her about the insignia on her knife handle. Then, she and I threw our saddles over our shoulders and together with Dolly we followed him deeper into the cave.

EMERGING FROM A CANYON, we took in a sunlit desertscape, scented by juniper and sage, stretching as far the eye could see. Vultures soared in a blue, cloud-streaked sky. Our wagon—snorting horses already hitched, breath steaming in the cool morning air—sat in the middle of the pebbled wash. The canvas had been repaired, and for a moment I worried that the Gatling had been ripped from its mount. But when I peeked behind the bonnet, the hand-cranked gun was still there, including ammo boxes, waiting patiently.

"I thought you were taking us to Rocker's wagon," I said. "This one is *ours*."

"Rocker and his men are on the other side of the

gorge," Ephraim said, indicating a split in the wall that evidently served as the last patch of sandstone before the open desert. "This is where I leave you, Kid." He extended his hand.

"Thanks for everything, Father," I said, coming in for an embrace, which he returned. "Hope we meet again. Let me know if you care to visit Virginia City."

"I'm no longer fit for civilization. The noise of mining equipment is the din of hell."

"Can't argue with you there."

"See you, Kid. Nellie?"

"Yes, Father Ephraim?"

He produced a crumpled paper sack with something in it. "Take care of this wild young man. He's hell on wheels, but his heart is pure."

"I won't let him leave my sight, sir. Holy sh— sorry, Father. Thank you so much for the extra cornbread!"

He smiled for a moment, then his grin faded. He brought his hands together and mumbled a blessing over us before making the sign of the cross. Then he abruptly turned around to walk back into his monastery of caverns.

"Goodbye, Father Ephraim," I said.

The Desert Saint didn't respond. Instead, he pointed enigmatically toward the sky, continuing on his way.

"A curious soul, that one," Nellie said, reaching into the bag for the cornbread. Hungry, Dolly stood on the tiptoes of her new sandals to reach for some. When Nellie noticed, she pulled the bread into two pieces, handing the bigger half to Dolly. The girl gnawed it ferociously.

I couldn't tell Nellie what I'd discovered in the cave, not until I understood why she had a knife that bore the seal of the Knights of the Golden Circle.

"We should get moving, Miss Nellie," I said. "Once we're done looking at the Mormon munitions factory and reunited with Colonel Connor's regiment, I need to pick up where I left off with Ustick."

"In what way?"

"Having a private conversation with him."

"I'd pay to be a fly on the wall for that one. Though I suspect there'll be *plenty* of flies drawn to the outcome of *that* discussion."

We got in the wagon, and made our way through the opening in the outer canyon wall, everything in the landscape cast in a warm glow. There was a majesty in our surroundings, petroglyphs carved in the sandstone walls all around us.

As we came around the corner, we encountered genuine horror—two Paiute scouts ransacking a horseless wagon, with two dead white men, faces on the ground, pincushioned with arrows and scalped.

The crunching of our wheels alerted the warriors to our presence, both reaching for their rifles inside the wagon bed. I was too far away to hit either of them with my pistol, especially since they had partial cover inside the wagon. I fired anyway, hoping to buy us a fraction of a second to find cover. Nellie and Dolly jumped off the buckboard and darted behind a boulder; I went the other way, sliding behind an outcrop of stones as Winchester rounds flew all around me. Miraculously, none of our horses were struck, even as gunfire encouraged them to pull the wagon to the edge of the ravine.

"Those two men shooting at us," Nellie called over to me, "don't look like anyone named Rocker Portwell."

"He's dead," I said. "Or his friends are. How's Dolly?"

"She's good. What's our plan?"

"Thinking I'll get closer to them, maybe scramble up this mesa behind me, since it offers some cover. Then I'll come around behind them."

"Someone got there first."

I looked back and saw she wasn't kidding. Leaping dramatically off the ten-foot overhang with a bear-like growl, a huge mountain man in denim and wool, holding a rifle at both ends, cannonball-crashed into the wagon bed, nearly flattening one of the Paiute and causing splinters to fly and the rear axle to snap. The impact knocked both warriors into the dust.

They tumbled into fighting stances, knives drawn.

The giant aimed his rifle, but it jammed when he pulled the trigger, probably from having slammed it against the wagon's brake lock. With a barbaric yawp, he tossed the weapon, then jumped from the wagon to charge the warriors.

The closer Paiute sliced him first, opening a cut in the giant's forearms. He ignored the pain and blood and grabbed the warrior's wrist and, with one sudden movement, yanked the arm out of its socket.

As the warrior fell to his knees in agony, the giant wrested control of the blade and shoved it into the warrior's throat.

The other warrior had already stabbed the giant's back, creating a spurting wound. The noise of the blade breaking human skin was grotesque.

The man-ogre tried to backhand-smash the Paiute and missed, toppling into the dust. The enemy pounced. By this time, Nellie was stoked by the sight of knives and blood. Before the warrior could plunge his dagger into his prone combatant, she came running at the warrior with two blades in reverse grips before springing onto a boulder and pushing off. When she landed, she dragged both blades into the warrior's neck. The Paiute screamed as his life ended.

Nellie was smiling with satisfaction until the giant—eyes blazing with rage, spittle on his beard—stomped toward her menacingly with the cracked wagon wheel in his hand.

"Wait, fool!" she said. "I just saved your miserable life!"

She wound up to throw a knife, but the giant hurled the chunk of wood, smashing her collarbone and knocking her flat on her back.

Then the bruiser raised a sharp wooden spoke to stab her. He froze, however, when he heard the hammer cock on my Colt. Sensing it pointing directly at his back, he stiffened and rolled his shoulders, gasping from exertion and his knife wounds as he waited for the bullet.

"Rocker," I said. "You need to calm down."

10

TOGETHER, NELLIE AND I WEIGHED 290 POUNDS, while Rocker Portwell easily cleared 300. I regretted not having Bad Jace with us; he would've provided more raw muscle to pit against the Samson of Utah, a man credited with more kills than Wyatt Earp. I didn't want to shoot Rocker for the same reason I didn't care to snuff Colonel Connor. Sometimes killing a man invited entire organizations to seek revenge. The last thing I needed was a blood feud.

After my discovery on one of her blades, Nellie, at least for the moment, was difficult to trust. But if this lumbering Mormon oaf touched a single hair on Dolly's head or inflicted pain on anyone I cared about back in Virginia City, I'd tuck him in for a long dirt nap. He didn't intimidate me. If I didn't have a gun, I'd find a way to kill him—even if he was a looming behemoth who shrugged off Paiute knife wounds.

He slowly turned to face me, boots crunching in the gravel, winding down his heavy breathing. "You're the

Kid," he said, voice lower than Dante's ninth circle. "Heard about you."

I slowly lowered my pistol. "And I hear you're our guide for the cannon forge you're operating in Goblin Valley. I say we bury these two friends of yours and get moving before more bandits arrive."

Rocker nodded, surveying the corpses around us. "I went to take a piss and get a view of the canyon. That's when the Paiute attacked my brothers. Elder Zachariah and Elder Hyrum were good men. The violence they suffered was awful. A peaceful death is preferable."

"There's no peace in the desert," I said, holstering my Colt. "Only punishment. And silver and gold, if you're strong enough."

Rocker grunted. "The so-called Desert Saint says you're an honorable man. I'm taking you to Goblin Valley only because we don't want the Union army upending our plans."

"I'm not a soldier, in case it's not obvious."

"Yes, but you know important men in Washington. And your predicament is…similar to ours."

"Similar to what the Mormons suffer? I don't see it."

"Like us, you're forced to choose sides," Rocker said, "for the sake of convenience."

What he said was true, but not the whole story. "I do what I do for money. Maybe *that's* the similarity."

He shook his head, squinted. "You're a lost soul, Kid. You seek a bandage that doesn't exist in this world. So you lash out."

"I'm the one who lashes out?" I pointed at Nellie, limping toward us and rubbing her shoulder. "Looks like you both require bandages—the *real* kind."

"Sorry I struck you, miss," Rocker said to Nellie. "Anger got the better of me."

"You nearly broke my neck," she said, still rattled by the blow. "I'm Nellie."

"Thank you for what you did for me, Nellie," he said, finally. "This your daughter?"

Dolly shyly approached, tears in her eyes. She looked once, twice, at the dead warriors, as if to confirm that they couldn't harm her. Then she ran at Nellie and jumped into her arms with a sob.

"Ouch! Girl, my shoulder is in a bad way." But Nellie held her tight as Dolly cried on her shoulder.

"Hear anything," I asked Rocker, "about a massacre?"

Blood pouring into his shirt, he said, "I know about it. Before I explain it, I need a little attention. It would be a shame to bleed to death in pleasant company."

I walked over to the wagon for my saddle and secured a bottle of carbolic acid and a toothbrush. Heading back, I scooped up a few dried-up limbs of juniper trees from the wash to build a fire.

"This will hurt, Mr. Portwell."

"I'm used to it," he said. "Don't skimp."

———

TRUE TO HIS WORD, he explained what he saw and didn't cry out as I scrubbed his wounds with the antiseptic, the sickly-sweet smell gagging me. According to Rocker, he and his buddies were on their way to Father Ephraim's cave, at the halfway point from Goblin, when midday heat turned to cool evening. They observed, from a hogback ridge, a caravan of threadbare wagons wobbling across the valley and along a trail that only Paiute and Ute used during winter months.

"See those mounted warriors on the dip slope?" Zachariah said to Rocker. "That's an ambush."

"Come on, those can't be Indians," Hyrum mulled aloud. "They don't sit right on their horses."

"They're whites," Rocker said, "dressed as Ute."

"Making it look like an Indian attack, you think?" Zachariah said.

Rocker nodded. He wondered if the attackers had seen him and his friends.

"How many are there?" Hyrum asked.

"I'd say ten." Rocker didn't like those odds.

They took cover behind a clutch of aspens as the pretend Ute on horseback howled and hooted their ersatz war cries. They raced toward the wagons, with the drivers slow to react, only managing to complete a half-circle that afforded no protection. Gunfire cracked, echoing across the valley along with screams of agony. The attack was merciless, ferocious.

Bullets rained down on the settlers sitting in the buckboards, hiding behind the covered wagons. Outnumbered and outmatched, the ones that tried to run were shot down like dogs. Women and children were dragged into the desert scrub and executed at point-blank range. From atop the tree-lined hill, Rocker heard their prayers, pleas for mercy and dying breaths, but there was no quarter, no salvation, no escape.

He sensed Elder Zachariah bristling, eager to intervene and throw in with the settlers, but everything happened too fast.

"There's no sense," Rocker said, "in the three of us taking on ten vicious murderers. The settlers have been wiped out to a man."

"This is *our* territory," Elder Hyrum pointed out. "We can't just let gentiles commit whatever atrocities they want here. Those settlers aren't Mormons, but they didn't do anything to deserve such cruelty."

Rocker nodded, wondering if he'd have to restrain one or both of his brothers. It didn't come to that; instead, they watched as the murderers dropped pieces of Ute clothing and weapons on the ground beside the bodies. Then one of them flint-ignited a piece of wood and set fire to the wagon bonnets, the bright orange flames burning against the bruised sunset.

The intent was clear, a massacre to be blamed on Indians.

When they were satisfied with the bloodshed they'd wrought, they mounted up and galloped away into the enveloping darkness, monsters returning to the void that spawned them.

"Check for survivors?" Zachariah asked, gloomily.

"There are none," Rocker said.

No longer visible in the night, the three of them untethered their horses, tired and hungry from a full day's ride, and continued on to Father Ephraim's monastery. Together, they descended the embankment that led to a hidden trail running parallel to the one the settlers had used.

"Look," Hyrum hissed at his brothers.

They turned to see a lantern light approaching the massacre site. As it came closer, it resolved into a lone wagon, an awkward crustacean scuttling across the sand, on the verge of a horrible discovery.

"Another settler?" Zachariah said.

Hyrum spurred his horse, pushing it to a canter, then a gallop, in the direction of the massacre.

"Wait!" Rocker shouted.

"We should follow," Zachariah said.

"Yes." Rocker sighed, shortened the reins, and yelled, "Hike!"

The dust Hyrum kicked up instilled anxiety in Rocker.

He couldn't make out what kind of wagon had rolled up to the flames, which had cast an eerie glow across a morbid tableau, causing the air to be thick with the stench of death.

It was a whiskey trader moving his product to Virginia City, while selling rotgut to a few tribes along the trail. He was sifting through what was left of the settlers' belongings. At one point, he dipped into a dead man's bloodstained jacket to take his watch.

"You're disgusting," Zachariah said to the whiskey trader.

"We should kill you right now." Hyrum, still on his horse, drew his pistol.

"Now hold on!" the corpse-robber insisted, raising his hands in the air. "A watch can't help this fella anymore. He's dead!"

"So are you." Hyrum cocked the hammer.

"Enough," Rocker said. "This place is cursed. Let vultures savor this fresh hell."

I interrupted the mad Mormon to tell him the whiskey trader had found more than a watch. He'd taken Dolly before Nellie and I met with him yesterday. "We had an argument," I said, finishing up with the suture on his back. "I won."

Rocker considered this, then flinched as I cut the thread with my teeth. "Seems I owe Dolly an apology too."

I shook my head, indicating we shouldn't discuss it. I asked him, "What brought you to Father Ephraim's caves? You didn't know I was coming."

He shrugged. "The Desert Saint works as an informal banker and financier. When we need materials, we borrow money from him."

"Where does he keep it?" I said, knowing the answer. "In the caves?"

Rocker glared, rotating his arm slowly to see if the stitches held. "Once you see our operation, you'll understand everything."

"How soon can we reach Goblin?"

"Two days. We should head out now while it's still morning."

"I'm ready," said Nellie, coming up to us, arm in a sling.

"You can't shoot or throw knives like that," I said.

"I can do all kinds of things like this."

Dolly clung to her leg, staring warily at the Mormon enforcer.

"I'm not going to hurt you, girl."

"She saw you wallop me. Can't trust a man that hits a woman."

"Hm. Is that how it is?"

Nellie didn't respond. She just limbered up her wrist attached to the hand that held a knife, the hand that wasn't clutching Dolly protectively.

"Let's cool our temperatures," I suggested firmly. "I'll make coffee, then we'll move out."

Rocker shook his shaggy head. "We don't drink coffee."

"Who's we?" Nellie said.

"Latter-day Saints."

"Why not?"

"It's against the Word of Wisdom."

"You must be a sleepy bunch."

"We're never idle. As for me, I don't sleep," Rocker said, regret in his voice. "Nightmares."

His statement quieted Nellie. We each dreamed the thin sleep of the ravaged.

While Rocker dug a hole in a patch of soft, deep, red shale and mudstone twenty yards away from the canyon, I cooked the coffee beans that I'd mortared with a rock. I also ground cocoa beans for Dolly, mixing it with salt and cayenne pepper, so that she could enjoy a hot chocolate. As I handed the mug to Dolly, I saw Rocker catching the scent.

"Can I have some?"

"You said you didn't drink coffee."

"Hot cocoa isn't coffee."

Nellie made a noise of disapproval and sipped her brew.

After making him his own chocolate, I said to Rocker, "I'll help you bury your friends."

We loaded the bodies on the wagon and carried them over to where Rocker had dug the hole. Then we dropped both corpses into the pit and covered it.

We removed our hats and stood silently beside the grave, until Rocker felt inspired.

"Lord, we pray this place will be hallowed and protected until the Resurrection."

"Amen," Nellie said.

Dolly got down on her bare little knees, put her hands under her chin, and bowed her head. "*Gott segne sei.*"

"She also speaks Swedish," Nellie whispered to me.

"That's German," I said quietly. "*God bless them.* Her parents were Lutherans."

Tears fell in rivulets down Dolly's face. I realized that she was saying goodbye not to the dead Mormon men, but to her parents, her family, her community. It was heartbreaking to witness and soon Nellie saw it too, covering her mouth.

Rocker slapped the dust from his hat against his

pants and walked over to Dolly. He reached out to touch her shoulder, then thought better of it. Instead, he said, "Don't worry, tiny one. We shall be reunited with all our beloved kin in the Last Days. Meantime, we must protect the cherished ones who remain."

"Yes." She sniffed. "I know."

As we climbed aboard our trail-weary wagon ferrying a Gatling gun, I assessed our misfit quartet—a Nevada gunfighter running from his brutal plantation past and hired on as a Union spy, a New Orleans knife thrower and voodooist who went west to join a circus and might be an agent of a Dixie conspiracy, a Mormon assassin building a weapons factory for his Utah-based religious cult that embraced plural marriage, and the sole-surviving Lutheran child of a massacre perpetrated by whites costumed as Indians. We comprised an odd group, each of us gouged by circumstances that we couldn't control. We had a common goal in our sojourn, however. We yearned to escape and find love in a world that wanted us dead, and we'd do nearly anything within our powers to come up with a way out of this mess. The sun climbed toward its apex in a bright blue sky and I thought of the quote in a book Poppy had given for my birthday, Sun Tzu's *The Art of War*: "Confront them with annihilation, and they will then survive."

We had encountered destruction at every turn so far and the four of us were still here. I could only hope to return to Virginia City from my mission in time to save my friends and loved ones from the furies of war and greed. It was the only reason I needed to keep going and, along the way, to eradicate as many deserving lunatics as necessary.

11

The first day's ride was tedious, a dust-choked galumphing across red rock formations sprinkled with lush pockets of greenery that soothed our sun-blasted minds. We'd filled our canteens from an aquifer that ran through Father Ephraim's cave monastery, but the heat kept us drinking and soon we were running dry and growing thirsty. Nellie sat between Rocker and me while Dolly dozed like an angel in the bonnet shade beside a metal-linked belt of 1,000 .31-caliber rounds.

"Let's stop in Silver Reef," I said. "Refill our canteens and maybe get a bite."

"I don't like that town," Rocker said. "It's not a friendly spot."

"We won't stay long. Besides, I'm expecting a telegram from Virginia City."

"Can't let you do that, Kid. I know Colonel Connor is searching for our munitions factory. You might alert him."

"Rocker, relax. Look at the size of you. You haven't eaten anything all day. I'll buy you a steak."

He pondered the offer, smacking his mouth. "Okay, but no telegrams."

I nodded, and minutes later we veered away from the main trail to take the Silver Reef route. As we approached the town, a storm cloud darkened the horizon—an ominous sign. Nellie yawned, having endured a restless night under the stars, disturbed by the sound of yipping coyotes and Rocker's snoring. At the moment, her head drooped as she closed her eyes, until the wagon hit another rock in the road, causing her to blink and rest her lovely head on my shoulder. I was exhausted too, having not slept in one of Grover's satin-lined coffins in nearly a week. I didn't mind catching winks outdoors; I always slept better when I was bone-tired from tracking and fighting. Spending all day with my butt on a wagon seat was mind-deadening, sure, but it didn't keep my brain from spinning at night, when dreams of fighting other kids in the Okefenokee for the entertainment of heinous men plagued me.

"They say," I said to Rocker, "that you grew up with Joseph Smith, the founder of Mormonism."

"He was like an older brother, and I looked up to him all my life," Rocker said. "I picked vegetables in the fields to help him pay for the first publication of the Book. I was sixteen."

"It's an open secret," I said, "at least among the Pinkertons and US Marshals, that Governor Thomas Ford ordered Smith's murder. Of course, Ford was already a lunger at that point."

Rocker turned his head to cough and spit phlegm. "I'd have happily killed the governor, but God took care of him for me."

"Think forging dozens of cannons will protect your church?"

"Inequity creates war. When one group seeks power over another, the result is violence. People have long sought to destroy us, and we're ready."

"Why side with the Union?"

"The South believes it has the right to own other men based on the color of their skin. If the Confederacy wins, what keeps them from enslaving Latter-day Saints?"

"Given what happened to your church in Missouri and Illinois, I wonder if you'd have better luck in, say, Dixie."

Rocker pshawed. "Southerners don't like blacks, Yankees, or Mormons. We'll take our chance with Lincoln, though the Union will need to negotiate with us."

As we turned onto the Silver Reef's main thoroughfare, I said, "I have no doubt about that. And I assume cannons are part of the negotiation."

He ignored my question. "It's been a while since I've been in Silver Reef. Doesn't look any friendlier."

Silver Reef had a reputation as the wildest whiskey stop in Utah, where Mormon families were abundant yet besieged by contentious miners who craved alcohol and whores. To the point that the Latter-day Saints didn't bother installing a church here. I'd only stopped in Silver Reef once before with my Paiute friend Snake, and though things went a bit sideways, we had an enjoyable time tussling with the local riff-raff and drinking ourselves to the end of a break-even game of poker at the Holy Moses saloon. I agreed with Rocker, though: Silver Reef looked grittier, worse for wear. The brothel ladies standing on the balcony possessed a despondent aura, while the newspaper office looked to have recently been subject to arson, its façade blackened by flames with the scent of smoke hanging in the air. There was no sign of a sheriff's office, no undertaker, no bank, no post office. The Holy Moses, however, was thronged, boisterous. The saloon had a sign that boasted: WE COOK STEAKS. I noticed, too, a telegraph station.

"The rudiments of civilization," Nellie said, "seem to be lacking."

"Well, the stable is open," Rocker said. "I suggest we leave the wagon and horses there."

I navigated us toward the livery and gave the young man working there a quarter to feed and water the horses. Nellie lay down in the wagon bed and wrapped a blanket around herself. Dolly was still sleepy, so I picked her up and carried her to the general store to pick out candy. Seeing treats sitting in glass jars—lemon drops, licorice, candy hearts, spruce gum, chocolate cherries—awakened her, making her eager to sample the treats.

"Take this," I said, giving her fifty cents. "Go wild."

"This— this is a lot of money, Mr. Crimson," she stammered.

"We have another day's ride to Goblin Valley. Make sure we have enough sweets to get there."

She gulped from the pressure of it all, then looked up at me to smile. "I'll choose something for you and Nellie. And for the Giant Man."

"Thanks," I said. "I'll be in the saloon for a spell."

"I'm tired of mushy beans," Rocker said, as we made our way to the Holy Moses. "Beef will improve my mood."

"First, I need to check for a message."

"No telegrams, Kid."

"Not sending, just receiving. Come with me."

He sighed and followed me to the station, a weathered, paint-peeled wooden structure nestled between a barber and a boarding house. Inside, a stocky, cigar-smoking man in a bowler hat sat behind a desk cluttered with coils of telegraph wire, stacks of papers, and dead potted plants being used as ashtrays. The telegraph machine was brass and made a constant tapping noise, indicating a message was being sent or coming in along the wire. A ghostly portrait of Abraham Lincoln hung on the wall behind the operator. The tobacco odor was robust.

I said to the agent behind the counter, "I'm Kid Crimson, and I'm expecting a message."

The man, puffing smoke in the air, scattered the papers on his desk, as if picking one at random. "Yes, sir, got it right here, sir!" When he found what he was searching for, he rolled a sheet of official Western Union letterhead into the typewriter and banged out the message. Then he ripped the sheet from the machine and handed it to me.

As I started to read it, I noticed Rocker looking over my shoulder and gave him the evil eye. Raising his hands with a snide grin, he took a few steps back.

The agent looked at me and then at Rocker, seeing an amusing couple. He laughed aloud.

Rocker stared at him. The man cleared his throat and went back to work decoding Morse.

The message was from Bad Jace and said:

TEACHER SAFE IN VC.
SPOKE WITH R.
FRENCH REBS IN UT.
WATCH YR BACK KID.

I stuffed the message into my coat and tipped the agent with a dime. The French Confederate warning lit a fire in my brain as I weighed the possibilities—until the agent called me back.

"Oh, Mr. Crimson, there's a second message, sir!"

It was even more intriguing:

CIRCUS ATTACKED NEAR RATTLEPEAK.
NO WORD ON SURVIVORS.
SNAKE SAYS REBS STILL IN VC.
BE CAREFUL KID.
LOVE V.

Snake must've paid a visit to the Blood Nugget and told my friend and employer Verbena what he'd seen in the desert. Rattlepeak was where Snake's girlfriend ran a bar, which he visited in between hunting trips. He also seemed convinced that Confederate sympathizers hadn't all been cleared out of Virginia City.

I wondered if the appearance of French Greybacks and the raid on a traveling circus were linked.

"Everything okay, Kid?" Rocker said.

"Yes," I said. "Let's get that steak I promised you."

Before leaving, I told the agent to hand over the code scripts, which I promptly tore to pieces.

THE HOLY MOSES was going like a house afire. The din of spinning roulette wheels, upright piano, braying drunks, and giggling hookers overwhelmed the senses, making the Blood Nugget resemble a Sunday church picnic. Funny enough, the chaos didn't bother Rocker, who quickly nabbed an open table and sat down.

I was about to join him when two men approached.

The taller one, smoking a cigarette, said, "We were sitting here."

"Not anymore," Rocker growled.

The man put both hands on the table, leaned forward, and blew smoke in the giant's face. "Peter Priesthood, this is a bar for grown men. Take your skinny boyfriend here and get moving." His friend pulled the empty chair from the table and went to sit in it.

Rocker rose from his chair, towering over the man whose hands seemed suddenly glued to the table. "I'm not going anywhere," he growled, "until I eat a steak prepared by this establishment."

The Holy Moses' satanic furor muted itself as the foolish drunk, in a tiny voice, said, "Yes, sir! I'll gladly pay for the meal."

Rocker smiled. "I just got through telling my friend Crimson here that Silver Reef seemed to have lost its courtesy. And here you are offering to buy us both steaks! Thank you, sir. Care to join us?"

"No—no thanks," the man said, struggling to gain his footing and to retain his pride. "I'll let the bartender know you men are hungry."

"Crimson," said the shorter man. "I know that name. You're the killer from Virginia City."

"From your nightmares. We want our steaks medium rare. With a side of boiled potato."

"I love potatoes," Rocker said. "And my young friend needs whiskey."

"And my old friend needs a hot chocolate."

Rocker laughed at this. "Yes. Steak and cocoa!"

The men scurried away, heading toward the bar to fulfill our order.

Rocker and I sat back down, and soon the noise of the

Holy Moses escalated again. A woman in a feathered dress sashayed over and plopped herself down in my lap. She smelled like catchpenny perfume, and I was irritated that I'd likely smell like cloying toilet water until my next bath. It made me sad, especially knowing how good my Poppy smelled without having to douse herself.

"You look young and fun," she said, her breath reeking of alcohol. "You remind me of the French nobleman who was here last week."

This pricked up my ears. "That French aristocrat you mention is my cousin."

She playfully slapped my arm. "You're French, too? You sound Southern!"

"I immigrated to Georgia when I was a child. How *is* my cousin these days?"

I glanced at Rocker, arms folded, one eyebrow arched.

"Camille Polignon? Oh, he's an utter gentleman, and *very* healthy. Is he really a prince?"

"He is, yes. We'd planned to meet right here in Silver Reef. Did he say where he was headed?"

"He and his men are on their way to visit—well, to visit a factory of some sort."

"His men. You mean his platoon."

"Yes. He loves his soldiers! He snuck out West with them on a federal prison transport. A man named Ustick helped him and they're headed to the middle of Utah."

Bastard Ustick helping a French Reb? The factory was likely Rocker's Mormon munitions plant. Rocker was listening now, and we shared a look of urgency.

The bartender brought whiskey and glasses to the table. "Sorry about the trouble, Kid. This is on the house."

"Thank you, sir!" Of course, the woman poured

herself a drink and glugged it before pouring another one, then a drink for me. "What's your name, ma'am?"

"Winifred, darling. Will you speak French to me?"

"Bien sûr, but after dinner. I'm famished." I took a sip of whiskey.

She pulled me close, both arms around my neck, and whispered in my ear. "In bed. French sounds better in the sheets."

I nearly spit out my drink. When the bartender returned with the steaks, I paid him three dollars, which was too much. But since we were walking out with the plates and whiskey, I figured I owed him. I gave Winifred a dollar to fetch another bottle. We were gone before she reached the bar.

Rocker and I wolfed down our ribeyes, gristle and everything. At the general store, we scooped up Dolly, who was carrying a paper sack. I woke Nellie and handed her my potato.

"Sorry, I ate my whole steak."

"Kid, I had the craziest dream," Nellie said.

"Was I in it?"

"Yes, you were riding an elephant into cannon fire."

"I'd never hurt a defenseless animal," I said, smiling.

"No, I guess not." She rubbed the sleep from her face and stared at the spud. "But we've seen you wallop the hell out of a bastard."

"I'm turning my life around, Nellie. From now on, I'm all sugar and sunshine."

"Learn anything from your telegram?"

"A lot. There's a French Rebel named Polignon causing problems in Utah."

Nellie went quiet. "Kid, you and I can handle anything that's thrown at us."

"Like candy?" Dolly handed me a stick of licorice.

"Mmm," I said, taking a bite. "I love candy."

Nellie measured me with her eyes. "What scares me is I don't believe you're actually drunk."

12

Some twenty miles south and east of Silver Reef was Goblin Valley, Utah. At the foot of Temple Mountain stood a series of saw and shingle mills, each with its own reservoir that held water flowing down from the hills. From these ponds ran a churning flume leading to a massive floodgate that, when opened, turned the wheels that fueled the mills. The water seemed perversely abundant, coursing through a deep gorge, giving the Mormons additional water power that was perfect for mining. Seeing all this made me wonder if what I'd suggested to Ralston was true—namely that he coveted this area and sought to transform it into a silver ore-processing facility. Mormons were never adept at mining for some reason. I suspected it had something to do with the disgusting side effects that digging for precious metals generated. Noise. Waste. Alcoholism. Mormons tended to be fastidious, and mining—slimy, unpleasant, insane business—was antithetical to their way of life.

"Impressive operation," I said to Rocker, our wagon

rattling and clanging down a road that sidewinded toward the town hall. "Seems ideal for any industry—even gunsmithing."

The Mormon enforcer nodded. "We're blessed to have secured this location. We had to fight for it, tooth and nail."

"You may have to fight for it again."

"Not if you deliver a good word on our behalf."

"Why me? I'm sure Lincoln's representatives are in touch with your church and your governor."

"They are. But the president has lost faith in Governor Harding and will replace him. Besides, no one knows the extent of our steelworks. If you successfully backchannel, we'll have these guns ready for the Union army by December."

"I heard a rumor," I said, careful not to reveal too much, "that the Rebels are involved with your munitions effort."

He smiled, wiping his mouth with the back of his hand. "In truth, Jefferson Davis extended an offer, but it was rejected."

"I know, you told me. The Latter-day Saints chose to align with the Union."

"That...and the logistics of shipping thirty-six cannons from Utah to Virginia on Confederate wagons and rails."

I couldn't help but laugh. "A daunting task."

As we drew closer, I noticed that people had gathered in front of the church facing the road. Men dressed in the same denim overalls as Rocker stood casually yet attentively, some of them carrying work tools—hammers, misery whips, scythes—as if they'd just come from the fields. A dozen young women dressed in white held baskets of fruits and flowers, and as we came over the brow of the hill the girls began to wave at us. A table adorned with pitchers of lemonade and drinking glasses and a roast chicken on a serving tray was set in a patch of green grass that ran along the gravel path. Clearly, our arrival today had been expected, and as I brought our wagon to a halt, I noticed that the Mormons were curious about the gentiles Rocker had invited into the valley.

Nellie and Dolly stepped off the wagon and were immediately swarmed by the women and given lemonade and pieces of citrus. The questions posed to us were respectful yet off-putting, as if Mormon girls hadn't seen anyone outside their community for years.

"Are you Danish?" one Mormon beauty asked Dolly.

"What Apache tribe are you a member of?" another gorgeous specimen asked Nellie.

"You look like a gunfighter," another Aryan pretty said to me.

Only Nellie answered right away, "I'm a thirsty black woman from New Orleans, so forgive me for stating the obvious. This place and you people are like an illustrated Bible for white children. What kind of yummy lemonade is this? It's lip-smacking!"

"It's the best," the girl with her hair in pigtails said, "because we make it with lemonade syrup. Okay, basically, what you do is you cook sliced lemons, sugar, water, and salt in a pan, then let it cool and mix it with fresh lemon juice."

"It's so good," Dolly confirmed, then licked her lips. Though I observed her enjoying the lemonade, she gradually withdrew and became quiet and went inward in the midst of all the community. I reckoned this was a scene not unlike what she'd imagined awaited her and her family when they reached the promised land. Now, surrounded by these young men and women who resembled her own kin, Dolly was reminded of the ugly fact that she was now an orphan in the wilderness.

"Want some?" a beautiful blonde said to me, proffering a glass. She looked like a sunflower and smelled like a delicious tangerine. "My name is Emma."

I was about to introduce myself when my tour guide interceded.

"This is Mr. Crimson," Rocker said to her. Then he addressed everyone. "Brothers and sisters, please serve Nellie and Dolly a bite to eat. I need to show my friend here the steelworks."

"Yes, Elder Portwell," the women said in near-unison.

The men said nothing, smiling as they returned to their work assignments—some heading to the sawmills, others walking toward a structure that was being built closer to the mountain.

Nellie's eyes narrowed at this response. Dolly giggled before swigging more lemonade.

"See you soon, ladies," I said, doffing my hat to the Sunshine Sisters.

"Don't encourage them," Rocker said, grabbing me by my shirt. He led me up an incline that brought us closer to the limestone steephead, where I imagined the blast furnace was roaring. "They're not married, and Emma would love nothing more than to convert you."

"What, you don't think I'm convertible?"

"I'm sure you're capable of corrupting her. I hear you're a real Lothario of the West."

"Inaccurate. I'm more of a violent libertine."

"Well, the aggressive part of you will love what I'm about to show you."

"No one seemed that upset over the deaths of Elders Hyrum and Zachariah."

"Those men were from a different church in Ohio. They were sent here to see the steelworks so they could develop one for themselves."

Before we reached the edge of the gorge, I heard the clamor of machinery and the hiss of steam. Then I saw a single plume of black smoke belched into the blue sky from a towering smokestack.

"It's real," I said, standing at the cliff face. "I can't believe it."

I instinctively removed my hat to view the ravine better, but also out of respect for what I was witnessing —a full-blown steelworks operation in the middle of the Utah desert.

Hammers clanged against anvils. Heavy machinery thudded and reverberated, with teams of Mormon craftsmen toiling and taking each gun through the manufacturing process, from the smelting of raw iron ore to the precise shaping of cannon barrels. The foundry's furnace roared with frightening intensity as molten iron flowed like liquid fire into crafted sand molds, the intense light casting a fierce glow upon the faces of the men working below. A blacksmith cross-peened the red-hot iron, while a machinist drilled and bored the barrel to exact specifications. Carpenters, meanwhile, fashioned sturdy gun carriages from seasoned oak. Another group of men toiled exclusively on cannon balls. Munitions building, like silver mining, was an ugly business, but Rockwell and his gang of Mormons made it look tidy, even picturesque. I counted the cannons—at least eighteen completed Napoleon guns that fired twelve-pound cannonballs lying in the shade of a tarp overhang, with what looked like six more in the works.

"That's a lot of firepower," I said. "Is it enough to turn the tide of war in favor of the Union?"

"It's enough to do many things," Rocker said. "As you can see, they're almost ready, and every single one of these guns is available for Lincoln to implement in his war to preserve the Union."

"Does Colonel Connor know you're building cannons for the Yankees?"

"He's aware. But through a spy in his regiment, we understand that he wants to take these guns without paying for them."

"What? You mean Lincoln seeks to appropriate them for the war and dispatched Connor?"

"See why I need you, Kid?" Rocker said. "Tell the White House the cannons are ready. Urge them to pay in gold and silver."

"Negotiating weapons deals isn't my forte," I said. "I'm better at armed security."

"Well, Kid, then help us bring these guns eastward to Kansas. The Union can drag them the rest of the way to whatever battlefield. Tennessee. Virginia. Wherever."

"Kansas is two states over from Utah. It's too big a job and would cost you too much."

"I'd be willing to give you twenty percent."

"What number are we talking about exactly?"

He picked up a long, desiccated cottonwood branch, using it to scratch a number into the dirt.

The number was significant, enough for me to buy a grapefruit orchard in Sonoma County.

"Okay," I said, shaking the Mormon monolith's brawler-grade mitt.

WE BATHED in the hot springs and had our clothes laundered before the evening festivities, much to the relief of our hosts who I'm sure considered pinching their noses given how trail-ripe we were. Relaxing with Mormons wasn't as difficult as I'd been led to believe. Sure, they didn't drink, smoke, or perform secular music like Chaparral's ex-Mormon girlfriend Rosie. But they were deeply musical people, with an ebullient spirit animating them at their core. Not surprisingly, too much was made about the polygamous aspect of their beliefs, when in fact every married politician I could think of kept at least one woman—often two and sometimes three—on the side, in apartments in Washington or, in the case of Nevada public servants, in rooms in towns like Virginia City. Unlike scandal-obsessed people who lived outside the community of Latter-day Saints, no one in Goblin Valley even mentioned plural marriage, nor could I identify which wives were paired with what husband. They seemed too busy, too determined, to tame the terrain of Utah to savor the hedonism of engaging in unorthodox marital configurations. As an avowed hedonist and sensualist, I found this disappointing.

Rocker's people were also annoying in their refusal to discern that Nellie wasn't an Apache warrior. I didn't argue with them, and neither did Nellie, opting to let them think what they wanted. Still, we had a lovely evening singing church hymns and folk songs around a campfire, cooking sausages over flames, and drinking lemonade. I furtively spiked mine with a flask filled with whiskey I'd received from the Holy Moses bartender back in Silver Reef. I poured more than a little into Nellie's cup of lemonade, and soon she, Dolly, and I added our howling to the lovely voice of Emma, whose beauty intensified in the firelight. She played fiddle and sang like an angel, and when the others took a turn on their instruments, she asked me to take a walk.

"Where are we going?" I said, inebriated. I stood up and followed her.

"Into darkness," Emma said, leading me over to a spot beside a hoodoo, a tall and intriguing spire of rock that seemed to sprout everywhere in this valley. "Where we can't be observed."

She pulled me close, her skin so pale that she glowed in the night like a beacon of safety. She wasn't a fashion paragon in her bloomers, puffy pantaloons under a short skirt. But her facial features were so alluring—dimples and blonde hair and bright blue eyes and perfect rows of white teeth—that I wanted to eat her like a piece of candy.

"Life's greatest joys are found in the family," she said. "I think I might find joy in starting a family with Kid Crimson."

Removing my hat and placing it on a rock, I kissed her neck oh-so-sweetly and said, "How do you feel about grapefruit?"

"Oh, I love citrus! We grow oranges here. But I haven't had a grapefruit since we left Salt Lake City last year."

"I'm buying a farm in Sonoma County, so I can be surrounded by grapefruits and oranges and tangerines." I kissed her throat and ear and brow as I listed each item, eager to taste her mouth.

"Sounds delicious. Need a wife to help you manage the day to day of such an enterprise?"

I went in for the kill, pushing my mouth into hers. "Are *you* married, Emma?"

"Not yet," she said, reciprocating my caress. "What do you know about our church?"

"Enough to know that you're perfect." I burrowed my face into her bosom and inhaled her womanliness, causing her to moan as she ran her fingers through my hair.

Suddenly, a burning torch was in our faces. "Emma," a voice spoke from the shadows.

"Elder Wilford," she said, unctuous with irritation. "Why are you investigating our whereabouts?"

"Cease your recruitment," Wilford said. "You're needed. The men want popcorn."

"Tell them to make it themselves," she said. "Mr. Crimson was telling me about his plans to be a citrus farmer in California."

"Grapefroosh," I said, slurring the word to make it clear I wasn't a threat. "And the navel orange will soon be a big deal. You can bet on it."

"You sound like a drunken reprobate," Wilford said, stepping forward in a manner that was supposed to be intimidating. "And not at all like a farmer." He was several inches taller than me, his muscles huge from working in the foundry.

"You sound," I said, "like a fool upset that the better man is stealing his girlfriend."

He shook his head. "Emma is my friend, and you'll stay away from her."

"Or what." I stepped between Emma and Wilford, my hands clenched.

He turned away, returning to the fire. Or so I thought.

He swiftly turned back to slap my face with a lack of ferocity that was, to me at least, alarming.

I was only slightly drunk and could've easily cleaned his clock. But I was more interested in getting information than getting bloodied or bloodying anyone in this Little Town of Sweetness. I took a lazy swing as he pushed his burning torch at me, the heat of it nearly scorching my skin.

I went to boot-stomp his foot, but I let him see me coming from a mile away and stepped back. As soon as I had planted my weight forward, he struck me from the side with a blow to the temple that smarted. Wilford had a few mild boxing chops.

Then I lunged to grapple with him. But he evaded and cracked me against my jaw. The impact from the blow hurt a little but not enough to make me reconsider my strategy.

"Your skills are good," I said, rubbing my jaw for dramatic effect. "I didn't know Mormons sported."

"We don't," he said, smirking with satisfaction. "I picked up some pugilism from sparring with Brigadier General Camille Polignac."

A name that oozed French nobility. I relaxed my fighting stance and asked: "Who's this Polignac fellow, Elder Wilford?"

Recognizing that I'd lost interest in trading punches, he rounded his shoulders and wedged the still-burning torch into a clutch of rocks and rolled down his sleeves. "He's a Confederate officer. Came through with his regiment last month. Knows a lot about fisticuffs and sword fighting."

"And cannons?"

"Wilford," Emma hissed at her brethren. "You're talking out of turn."

He waved her away. "He made an offer, but Rocker insists it wasn't sufficient. Besides, our church doesn't stand for slavery. We believe in the Union."

"Where did Polignac head after Rocker spurned his offer?"

Wilford shrugged. "I assume back to the South."

"You said he's leading a Confederate regiment?"

"Yes. You know, because you asked, I recall him saying something about the Ute."

"What about them?"

"Something about studying them in their natural habitat."

"I bet," I said, realizing I needed to wake up early and send a telegram to Ralston from Silver Reed. "Wilford, you hit me so hard that I see the light now. Join me for a lemonade?"

"Glad to hear it," he smiled. "I can always go for a lemonade. There's boiled rhubarb pudding too!"

"Sounds delicious," I said, walking toward the campfire, Wilford joining me.

"Are you two," Emma said, downcast, "not going to finish fighting over me after all?"

13

EVENTUALLY, THE FESTIVITIES ENDED, THE Mormons providing Nellie and Dolly and me a clean cabin with three neatly made beds with a single candle illuminating the space. I was exhausted from traveling a great distance and sipping whiskey-laced lemonade, and getting punched, so I removed my hat and boots and tucked in fully dressed and without updating Nellie on what Elder Wilford had shared. Drifting behind the veil of sleep, I heard her encouraging Dolly to put on a cotton nightgown. Then they knelt beside Dolly's bed and recited the Lord's Prayer together.

It crossed my mind that, to the outside world, the dynamic between the two was akin to a plantation servant caring for her white owner's child. Of course, that wasn't the case here. I was learning about the depths of Nellie's heart, her empathy for others despite the abuse she'd endured. I couldn't account for the Knights of the Golden Circle brand on her blade, but her compassion was easily explainable; she was someone who recognized the ache in others, doing her best to salve their wounds and be of service to those who had nothing. If I examined her objectively, Nellie didn't join me on this adventure for money. She saw something familiar in me, something she recognized in herself—a lust for danger in a world that promised subjugation and menace. Better to turn yourself into a living weapon than be threatened by the guns of fools. She reminded me, too, of my beloved in Georgia, a beautiful slave my father murdered before my eyes to break my spirit and force me to enlist in his repulsive mission to dominate the South.

It didn't work. The evil he conducted had summoned a revengeful monster he didn't anticipate, a creature so depraved that I scared myself recalling the deaths that resulted. I carved a bloody swath from Georgia to Nevada to escape. What I found in Virginia City was hardly better, but the West offered me a chance for renewal, and Poppy offered me a chance to live a life other men could only fantasize about. But I needed Nellie's help.

I was too tired to tell her all this, so, lying in my bed, I said, "Nellie, thank you."

"Uh-oh," she said. "You don't sound well. I noticed your shiner. Care to explain?"

I yawned, remaining flat on my back. "No, just worn out and feeling sorry for myself."

She approached my bed, and for a moment I thought she intended to get under the sheets. Instead, she looked down at me, stroked my cheek. "You look like a kid, Kid."

"I'll never grow up," I said, smiling, taking in her beauty. "Adulthood is for the dogs."

She stooped to kiss my brow, just as my mother did when I was a child with a fever.

I heard the scampering of little feet from across the

room, and soon Dolly showed up to smooch my cheek. Then she scampered back to her bed. "'Night, Kid!"

Nellie laughed and, before climbing into her own bed, blew out the candle.

"Goodnight, Kid," she said.

I used the sheets to dry the tears on my bruised face. "Goodnight."

I SLEPT a few hours before waking up, bolt upright. There were sounds in the night that I didn't like, dreadful noises of conspiracy and malevolence. Whispers of moccasined feet, men creeping past our cabin on their way to the steelworks. Faint clattering of bullets inside a rifle chamber. Breathing of saddled horses and armed assailants striving to remain undetected.

But I detected them. After all, I was born in the Deep South, where boys learned to identify birds by the vibration of wings in the air and to pinpoint snakes by the slithering of scales across leaves and moss. I sensed a conspiracy underway. I slipped on my boots, donned my hat and gun belt, and stirred Nellie.

"Someone's here," I said quietly, placing her knife belt and boots on the edge of her bed.

"Okay," she said. "Where's Dolly?"

"Asleep. They're not here for us. They're heading toward the steelworks."

"Saboteurs, I bet. Johnny Reb."

"Maybe. But I hear the swish of animal pelts and jewelry. Not wool and buttons."

"What? Kid, you can't possibly hear anything like that."

"Hush," I said. "Let's follow the shadows."

We left Dolly sleeping in her bed, following the scent of the intruders down to the steep, rocky walls of the gorge, where the cannons forged by Rocker's men sat.

"The odor of these trespassers," Nellie said, "is familiar."

"They sound like Ute, but smell like unwashed white men," I said.

We continued tracking them. I wished I'd paid better attention to the site of Rocker's quarters. I considered doubling back to fetch him, but I didn't care to risk the possibility of retreating as the steelworks was being sabotaged. Nellie and I pressed on, following the trail deeper into the darkening gorge, past a cascading waterfall that tumbled down sheer cliffs, echoing off the canyon walls. With each step, the air grew cooler.

"They're up ahead," I said.

"How can you tell?" Nellie asked.

"Their guns are trained on us." I shoved her behind a slope of shale, then dove behind a mudstone deposit.

Glinting in the desert moonlight, a rifle blasted in our direction from thirty yards away, a volley of bullets tearing into the rocks and trees around us.

A bone-chilling Ute battle cry pierced the darkness, causing Nellie to scratch her head.

"No, they don't even *sound* like Ute," she scoffed.

There was the crack of gunfire deeper in the gorge. I figured that Rocker's security detail had encountered the intruders, and the fight was on.

"Let's go," I said to Nellie. "We need to back them up."

"Kid, wait!"

I went charging through dense scrub and sandstone that ran parallel to the trail until, from my blind spot, a rifle butt stopped my headlong momentum. It crashed against my spine, sending me into a patch of loose sand. I reached for my pistol, but it was gone, no doubt dislodged by my fall. When I slowly stood up in the lantern light, I found myself face to face with the enemy, a man that I'd hoped to encounter again and punish severely for his mistreatment of my close friend, the Virginia City piano player Chaparral.

Dressed in tanned deer hides adorned with beadwork and feathers, Private Ustick stood before me, rifle in one hand and the lantern in the other, his simpering grin making me want to puke.

"Well, aren't you just a peach," I said. "You know, Ustick, that's the garb of an Indian warrior, not a saboteur."

"The Mormons will blame the Ute," Ustick said. "Colonel Connor and his regiment can chase Indians and secure prison transports to his heart's content."

Ustick had been assigned to guard prisoners and ended up scalping some of them, which is what he'd shared with Lydia Sweet in a disgusting attempt to impress her. "You're a deserter and a fiend," I said, "on top of all your other deficiencies."

"I received a better deal. You understand the temptation. Union infantry pay isn't much."

I carefully nestled the toe of my boot under a rock on the ground, hoping for an occasion to punt a stone at his head and wrestle the weapons from his grip. "I don't understand fools. They never learn their lesson until it's too late."

"I'd love to spend time chatting with you, Kid," he said, leveling his rifle at me as three other whites dressed as Ute emerged from the darkness to join us. "But my fellow knights and I have a Union foundry to wreck."

Knights. Did he mean the Golden Circle? "Ustick, one last question."

"Sure, Kid."

"Why does your mother keep coming back for more?"

He laughed. "I promise not to mutilate your corpse. I'll reserve that pleasure for your negress."

Two more fake Ute warriors staggered into the cast of the lantern's light, dragging Nellie with them, arms tied behind her back, her face a mask of shame. "Shoot them, Kid!" she said. "Don't worry about me!"

"Lost my gun, Nellie," I said, making peace with my death. As a gunfighter, I'd accepted that living a long, abundant life wasn't in the cards.

Suddenly, there was a loud explosion from the base of the gorge. When the blast and its echo died down, men's shouting reached my ears, sounding like they were heading our way. I could only assume the Mormons were mobilizing to chase down the perpetrators.

A bear-like growl interrupted what I figured to be my last ruminations before falling to a hail of bullets from Ustick and his cronies. In the gloom, I saw Rocker leaping from the lower rim of the pitch-dark canyon, smashing into the ersatz Ute like a bowling ball breaking a set of pins. Ustick's rifle went off, a sudden spasm of light. I didn't know if the shot connected with anyone else, but I did know that it didn't rip through me. I boot-scooped the rock into my hand and hurled it like a baseball into his chest, knocking the wind from him, his desperate gasps like music to my ears.

Nellie, meanwhile, reverse head-butted one of the men restraining her, then shin-racked the other with her boot, causing him to fall over the cliff and plummet into the gorge below us.

Muzzle flashes, but it seemed that Rocker had

wrenched a gun into the air, keeping the barrel from pointing at him. He mule-kicked another assailant off the cliff, screaming to his death.

At this point, Ustick dropped the lantern, which crashed against the rocks. When it extinguished, we were plunged into darkness. I couldn't tell with whom I was trading punches, but as my eyes adjusted to moonlight, I saw Ustick crumpled in the dirt, clutching his sternum in agony as the impostor Indians disappeared, scampering up the ridge where their horses were waiting.

"Cut me loose," Nellie said, her arms still tied.

I drew my Bowie and slashed her binds, freeing her. She immediately took off running, calling "Dolly!" over her shoulder.

When I looked for Rocker, I found him choking the last remnant of life from one of Ustick's co-conspirators. There was a hideous death rattle.

"Rocker," I said. "Enough."

He seemed to instantly awaken from a nightmare, looking around with concern as if he didn't recognize his surroundings. He made me think of a berserker from the age of Vikings.

"The steelworks," he growled. "We need to assess the damage."

I located the lantern Ustick had dropped, reigniting the wick with a match I kept in my gun belt. In seconds, I retrieved my pistol. "I'll go with you," I said.

As we made our way deeper into the gorge, we smelled the stench of sulfur, hot metal, and gunpowder. The explosive they used was significant, and the foundry resembled a smoking ruin blown apart by ordnance. The Mormon men were on site now with lanterns and torches, casting onto the devastation, and as we examined the puzzle in the darkness, I observed Rocker's anger and frustration.

"We were so close to finishing," he muttered.

"It gets worse," Elder Wilford said, walking up with a torch.

"What do you mean?"

"Three of the finished cannons are missing."

"Exactly how in the name of our Holy God," Rocker said, "did they pull three heavy Napoleon cannons out of this gorge?"

"Well, if you recall, Elder Rocker, we were testing the wheeled carriages—"

"And so they simply pulled them up the trail," I said, looking at the tracks that went up the path on the canyon's other side, "with mule teams."

Elder Wilford nodded. "They took the cannons before they blew up the foundry. Elder Palmer suffered a bout of the trots during his shift and—"

Rocker raised his fist at Elder Wilford, indicating that he should stop talking.

"You still have eighteen cannons," I said.

"I promised Lincoln thirty-six."

"Ustick is part of a Confederate cabal," I said. "We should interrogate him and learn more. We'll drop him off at Fort Union, where they'll try him for conspiracy. Lincoln will appreciate your efforts."

Rocker stared at me for a long moment. "Take Elder Wilford with you when you speak with Ustick. Our young farmers should learn how to respond to a violent world."

"I— I already know how to respond," Wilford said. But of course, he had no clue. He was a nurturer of the earth and a provider, not a brazen killer like Rocker and myself.

Elder Wilford and I returned to where we'd struggled with Ustick and, to our dismay, found him dead with Nellie's knife buried in his heart. It was the blade that bore the stamp of the Knights of the Golden Circle.

"Obviously, you didn't stab him," Wilford said.

"No. I know who did. But I don't know why."

14

Elder Wilford and I returned to the cabin to find Dolly peacefully sleeping, unharmed. Our wagon and horses were still in the Mormon livery, but Nellie was nowhere to be found. Returning to the scene of the violent encounter, we scanned the prints on the ground. It was impossible to pick out Nellie's boot tracks, given how frenzied the encounter had been.

"Maybe she stabbed Ustick," Wilford said, "then ran away."

I thought about it. What would she run away from? No, she was taken. "She killed him in the process of getting herself kidnapped."

"By whom?"

"These fake Ute warriors and whoever is funding their campaign of terror." I suspected they were financed by the Knights of the Golden Circle or even the Confederacy. "Elder Wilford, I have to speak with Rocker. Do me a favor and ask him to meet me in the stable."

"No need," Wilford said. "Here he comes now."

Breathing heavily, Rocker came stomping up the trail from the gunpowder-wrecked gorge. "We need to see Father Ephraim. Rebuilding the steelworks will cost money."

"They took Nellie and the cannons and blew up your foundry. I'll be pursuing the bastards shortly."

Rocker noticed Ustick's corpse. "She didn't leave without a fight."

"Judging by their tracks," Wilford said, "I'd wager they're heading in the same direction we are...back to Graves Valley."

I placed my boot on dead Ustick's chest and stooped to rip out the knife before cleaning it in the dirt. "Rocker, you should join me. I can't allow those lunatics to keep Nellie."

He looked at me, scratching his bushy beard. "I want my cannons. I'll help you find Nellie if you retrieve our guns."

"As I said before, it's a deal."

Another elder came running from the row of cabins near the upper creek where the Mormon families lived. Winded, he gasped for air, leaning on his thighs to catch his breath before speaking. His face was sweaty and panicked.

"Elder Spencer," Wilford addressed him. "What have you found?"

"Emma!" he exclaimed. "They've taken my sister!"

Wilford looked stunned, but his expression quickly became resolute. Two hostages now.

"Looks like you have even more reason to accompany us," I said to Rocker.

"I'm going with you too."

The Mormon enforcer suddenly gave Wilford a hard shove, nearly knocking him over. "You'll stay here and protect our congregation! You know what happened to Elders Hyrum and Zachariah."

"I'm done protecting!" This time Wilford stood with his feet planted, shoulders rolled forward. "You told me yourself that I must learn how to react to a world in flames. Well, this is how I learn—by rescuing Emma from the clutches of evil men."

"Same goes for me," Elder Spencer said. "She's my flesh and blood."

"That might be all that's left of her when we find her," I said. "Are you prepared for that?"

Spencer's Adam's apple bobbed with uneasiness. "Yes. We're prepared for what we'll find."

"And what we might have to do to avenge her," Wilford stated.

Rocker and I nodded at each other.

"All right, my friends," I said. "Either of you heard of a Gatling gun?"

———

I DID my best to explain that Nellie had been taken by bad people. Dolly asked if they were the same ones who murdered her family.

I didn't want to lie to her. "Yes."

"Then she's dead," Dolly said, holding her face in her hands.

I picked her up and held her as she sobbed into my shirt. It took a few heartbreaking minutes for her racking wails to subside.

From my saddlebag, I pulled out a handkerchief.

She blew her nose. "Kid, I don't want to see Nellie dead."

"You won't have to, Dolly. I feel her presence out there and you can too."

"Yes," she said, nodding. "They've got her tied up."

"We'll untie her. And she'll be so happy to see you."

She said nothing as I climbed into the buckboard and grabbed the reins. Staring at sunrise on the horizon, she wiped her runny nose.

"It's the color of a peach," she said. "Or a soft orange."

"Yes, but that's not where I'm headed."

She turned around to peer in the other direction. "Dark that way."

"Only in the morning," I assured her, sipping from the coffee I'd made for myself. "Before nightfall, the west will glow like it does now in the east. And then the east will be dark."

"So the sky will be the color of peaches," Dolly said, "when you rescue Nellie."

"And Emma," I said. "Don't forget Emma."

"She gave us chicken and lemonade."

"Yes."

"They both tasted so good."

That reminded me. "Are you hungry? I have a warm biscuit that Elder Wilford gave me."

"Please!"

I handed her the entire biscuit, wrapped in cloth.

She took a bite, chewing slowly, savoring. "Do you think Rocker will let me live here and join the Mormons?"

"I don't see why not. They all have big families. What's one more little snot-nose?" Her giggle bore right into my heart, but I smiled to hide it. "Here's another idea. I have friends for you in Virginia City, too, Ezra and

Sarah. They shine shoes for money and a few weeks ago they attended the circus and ate peanuts and popcorn."

She repeated their names aloud as if conjuring them into existence. "They sound nice. Promise you and Nellie will come back for me? Promise?"

"Yes, sweetheart. I promise."

Before I slapped the reins, she bowed her head, placed her biscuit-crumbed hands together, and said a prayer.

It was a touching scene, until I heard Dolly mumble a German word I hadn't heard in years.

Rache.

Vengeance.

I WAS JUST about ready to move and say my final goodbye to Dolly when my friend Snake, a Paiute warrior from Nevada, arrived on top of a horse I'd given him when I'd stopped in Rattlepeak last year. He was a sight for sore eyes...until I saw the animal that his blonde, fair-skinned, Spanish girlfriend Estrella Matero was riding. Estrella had threatened to kill me the next time she saw me and here she was atop a colossal elephant from Circus Southwest, the one Ezra and Sarah had fallen in love with under a big top propped up next to the Chinese graveyard in Virginia City. Sitting in a bamboo carriage positioned on the back of the elephant was Estrella, holding a large parasol above their heads, shading them from the sun.

The Mormon men sprang into action, picking up rifles and pitchforks as soon as the oversized pachyderm thundered into view, the earth trembling beneath its tree-trunk legs. Clearly, there was no chance Rocker's men planned to let Snake and his friends near their church.

"Relax, everyone," I said. "I know these people and I'm a huge fan of the elephant."

"I, however," Estrella said, surly-faced, "am *not* an admirer of Kid Crimson."

"I've been told I can grow on skeptics."

"Like fungus on a mummy."

"Wonderful to see you, too, Estrella. Snake, I received Verbena's telegram. What she didn't explain was that you're now caretaker of a busted-up circus."

Snake laughed. "I like circus people, Kid. They harness the power of magic."

"Must take sorcery," Rocker said, baffled, "to keep an animal that big hydrated in Utah."

All of us watched in amazement as the elephant dipped its trunk into the trough, sucked up water, and sprayed it into its mouth. It was a majestic creature, thirteen feet tall, its frame cloaked in wrinkled, charcoal-gray skin, massive ears flapping gently and cooling its body. The trunk was versatile, curious; its tusks, elongated ivory spears, enhanced the animal's allure.

"What's the sex of this elephant, Snake?"

"See for yourself. Definitely male."

"What's his name?" Dolly said in a lilting voice.

"Hannibal," Estrella said, cooling herself with a Chinese fan. "Little mama, I hope you're not one of Kid's carelessly spawned offspring."

Dolly furrowed her brow. "My parents are dead, killed by fake Indians."

Estrella opened her mouth to speak, then displayed a modicum of shame and refrained.

"About that," Snake said to me. "There's a secret brigade running amok in Utah, destroying everything in their path, including Circus Southwest. I got word of you heading to Goblin from Verbena when Estrella and I were passing through Virginia City. On the way here, we found Hannibal wandering the desert."

"Who's leading the brigade, Mr. Snake?" Rocker said.

"A French nobleman called Polignac, a general in the Confederate army, is now in the Southwest, having recently won a battle in Texas against the Union. But he's not wearing the butternut uniform," Snake said.

Rocker nodded. "He showed up here asking to buy our cannons."

"Polignac and his men are masquerading as Ute," I said. "He's siphoned men from Colonel Connor's Union regiment. Also, they stole cannons from the Mormon steelworks here in Goblin and smashed the foundry."

Estrella guffawed. "Let me guess, Kid. You were here when it happened."

I ignored her, focusing on Snake. "Rocker and I are off to find them. They took hostages."

"Have you wondered what they plan to do with the cannons, Kid?" Snake asked.

"Briefly. Dragging them all the way to Shenandoah seems Sisyphean."

"Thought about what they might be used for in Nevada, Kid?"

"Yep, blowing up the silver mines."

Snake smiled, nodding slowly.

Rocker groaned. "Kid, if they use Mormon cannons to flatten Virginia City, Lincoln won't be content to break the South. He'll come for the Latter-day Saints next."

I was already juggling a few ideas about how to defend the silver mines, but one notion was percolating deviously in my brain.

"Furnace burning again?" I said to Rocker.

"Yes, but all the cannon molds are shattered. It'll take weeks."

"What molds do you have?"

"The one we used to make armor plates for stagecoaches."

"Let me chat with the foundry guys before we go. Also, tell the women to measure Hannibal."

"Kid," Rocker said, scratching his bald head. "You're too much."

"He's too much nonsense, if you ask me," Estrella lamented.

Dolly had had enough, pointing her finger at the source of negativity. "Lady, you're a meanie!"

"I work in a saloon, little mama. Meanness is my protection."

"Well then, I'll never work in a saloon. I will work in a candy shop."

"Honey, that's what a saloon is. A candy shop for adults."

"Candy isn't good," Dolly said, "for some people."

Snake gave a laugh, then abruptly swapped it for a cough when Estrella glared.

———

IN THE WAGON, I tagged after Rocker, Wilford, and Spencer on horseback, their sorrels radiating health and vitality in the sun. Indeed, the three of them looked proud, capable, even if I was sure Spencer and Wilford lacked the killer instinct. Naturally, it didn't matter, since Rocker was the equivalent of ten stone-cold killers. I hadn't seen him shoot, but I sensed he took to a rifle, as the Southern expression went, like an opossum eatin' a sweet tater. The stock on his Winchester was worn, notched with kills, the gun emanating lethality. If we were up against an outfit of Union deserters or galvanized Rebels, I had no doubt Rocker would display uncanny sharpshooting skills. I didn't envy the men we pursued. Beyond my personal beef with them, they'd robbed the Mormons of their usefulness to President Lincoln, which, given the historical tension between the US and the late Joseph Smith, was a blow to the church. Heads would soon roll.

Judging by the freshness of the tracks, however, our prey didn't seem concerned.

"They're less than a mile ahead of us!" I called out to Rocker. "They're not in a hurry."

He brought his horse to a halt, so I could catch up with the wagon. "I'm concerned. Notice where they're headed?"

"Father Ephraim," I said. "He knows the canyon better than anyone. I doubt they'll find him."

"Sure, but what if they pay him to hole up there. We'll never reach them."

"They have the cannons, which Father Ephraim knows you're building. He's paying for the cannons. He won't hide Polignac."

"There's also a chance," Rocker said, "that they'll simply use the creek on this side of the valley to refill canteens and water horses."

"Exactly. Which is why I plan to draw them in and smash them. Of course, it involves you wearing women's clothing."

Mouth agape, Rocker looked at me. When he found his voice, he said, "Do I look like I can even fit inside a dress?"

I laughed. "You need to wear a large brimmed bonnet crown and a gingham drape. They're in the wagon bed."

"Kid," Rocker said. "I noticed you spiking Emma's lemonade with alcohol. I can't abide your drunken strategy to rescue her and Nellie while intoxicated. I might shoot you in the crossfire."

"I'm sober as a judge. My plan will work, as long as your thespian skills are sharp."

By this time, Wilford and Spencer had slowed their horses to eavesdrop on our conversation.

"What did he call you, Elder Rocker?" Spencer said.

"Equestrian, I think," Wilford explained.

Rocker winced at this before saying to me, "Let's make one of them do it."

"Sure," I said. "As long as I aim the Gatling."

"The gun you showed us?" Spencer said. "Bet it's loud."

"Not as loud as the screams it induces."

Rocker closed his eyes and shook his head disdainfully, then gazed up at the sky and said aloud, "With every fiber of my being."

"Talking to the Big Man?" I said, slapping the reins so that the wagon started moving again.

"Just can't figure," Rocker said, smiling, "why He put me in contact with you."

"I'd ask Him the same if He were listening."

"What complicated your faith, Kid?" Elder Spencer asked, bringing his horse to a trot.

"Organized religion in the South."

"Will you pray for my sister at least?"

"I never stopped praying. I still believe in God. It's God who doesn't believe in me."

The three Mormons made no response, offered no sympathy or pity. Instead, they spurred their horses onward and over a wheel-rutted trail.

The sky turned the color of peaches.

15

We caught up with them easily, spotting them as they made camp beside a shallow creek in front of a red sandstone cliff. Hidden within the shade of a cluster of pinyon trees atop a butte, gnats swarming our faces, we watched Polignac and his crew water their horses and cook beans. The descending sun began to tease orange and pink hues from a smattering of clouds on the horizon.

"I count forty men," Rocker said, looking through his spyglass. "How many do you see, Kid?"

"Same," I said.

"Where are the women?" I detected that Wilford was struggling to keep his composure. "Think they killed them?"

"At the moment," Rocker said, "they're likely in the back of that covered wagon."

Wilford exhaled his displeasure. "So what's the plan?"

"You're putting on a bonnet and driving up to their camp."

Wilford rubbed his forehead. "I don't want to get shot wearing women's clothes. Not in front of Emma."

"If you rescue Emma dressed like that, for the rest of her life, she'll believe you're the bravest man who ever lived."

Rocker had plunged a sharpened stick into a prickly pear and popped it off a cactus pad, knife-shaving the spiny hairs that grew on the outside of the fruit before slurping the meat. "I'm starting to like this plan. If you wheel the wagon past that hoodoo, the one twenty yards from their site, I can use it for cover and hammer them with a repeating rifle."

"The wagon is in the line of fire," Wilford pointed out.

"Not when you draw them to you," I said.

"What makes you think they'll attack? They're dragging cannons to Virginia City."

"I know they will because I can smell their wretched food from here. That's why I asked Elder Spencer and Dolly to paint those words on our canvas covering."

"'Chuck wagon,'" Wilford repeated.

Rocker chuckled. "Their food does reek something fierce."

"This plan is madness," Wilford said. "My life is going to fade away like the sun."

We slid down the dusty embankment behind the butte, where Spencer was soothing the horses, and prepared ourselves for engagement. I stepped up and into the tarp, priming the Gatling with the metal belt of ammunition while Wilford donned the honeybee bonnet, covering his body and his Winchester with the gingham drape, under which he also held the reins. Rocker hopped into the rear boot of the wagon with his Henry rifle across his lap.

"What if this doesn't work?" Spencer said.

"Head straight to Goblin Valley on those horses," I said. "Then, Elder Spencer, you're entirely on your own."

"Move out, Elder Wilford." Rocker's voice went low, suggesting he was ready to unleash havoc.

Wilford made a clicking noise, and the bay horses obeyed. Soon we were bumping and lurching over rocks and creosote shrubs, heading toward the camp of men who'd kidnapped our friends.

"Kid," Rocker said, gripping the wagon bow to keep from losing his balance. "I need to ask you something."

"Go ahead," I said.

"I told Spencer and his wife to raise Dolly as their own if we don't make it. Hope that's okay."

"It is. But I fully expect to bring her to Virginia City and use my law enforcement contacts to locate any family she might have out east or in Sweden."

"Good," Rocker said. "I think you're right. It's not our time to die."

THEY CAME GALLOPING AT US, wielding guns and hatchets and shrieking their fake battle cries. The hair on the back of my neck stood up as I watched Wilford begin to stand up in the buckboard.

"Stop!" I warned him. "Remember the plan. Turn the wagon in the opposite direction. Rocker, time to run!"

Rocker leaped off the back of the wagon and sprinted toward the rock formation as Wilford spun the wagon around so that I was now facing the oncoming rush of eight mounted soldiers.

Two of them veered off, heading toward Rocker's

position. That left six of them for me to mow down with the hand-cranked gun. Once again, I used my Bowie knife to slash away the tarp, which fell away like a curtain to reveal the mechanized death of a Gatling cannon.

Initially, I was concerned that I couldn't see anything from all the dust Wilford had kicked up in turning the wagon 180 degrees. But the wind carried it away, and I watched as the riders yanked on their reins, their expressions agog as they quickly realized they'd been galloping headlong into a wall of flying lead. They were too late to change course.

I rotated the crank, sending .58 caliber rounds, 200 per minute, three per second into their war-painted and feathered bodies, blasting them off their saddles. My teeth rattled in my skull from the recoil and noise. Hot bullet casings clattered all around me. Wilford ripped away his bonnet, hitting them with rifle fire. Somehow, we avoided hitting any horses, which gave me pleasure as I watched men careen into the dust.

The other two who sought to pursue Rocker doubled back, which was a mistake. Rocker coolly picked them off with his scoped Henry, one of the dead men getting his foot caught in the stirrup, his dead body trawling through sand for more than a hundred yards until it finally came loose.

I went to raise my fist to share a victory salute with Rocker, but I noticed him springing back behind the hoodoo for cover. I turned to look and saw that the platoon of Rebs had pushed forward the three stolen Mormon cannons, loaded and aimed and facing the enemy, which was us. The fuses were sizzle-smoking.

"Elder Wilford," I said, jumping off the wagon. "Run like the devil's on your tail."

"Please, Lord, no," he said, darting for the butte, hundreds of yards away.

The detonations were near-simultaneous.

THE CANNONS ROARED TO LIFE, smoke plumes billowing as they unleashed deadly payloads.

Out of the corner of my eye, I saw the top of the hoodoo shielding Rocker blasted to particles from the strike of a twelve-pound ball of iron. That was mere seconds before the wagon, Gatling mounted inside it, took a direct hit, exploding into a hail of wooden splinters.

Rocker lay flat on his stomach as the third cannon fired, gouging another huge chunk of rock from the hoodoo. The mushroom cap of the formation began to teeter and fall, with Rocker having to log roll to keep from getting crushed.

I was caught in the open, having at first decided to share Rocker's cover, but as the cannon blasts whittled it down significantly, I dashed in the same direction as Wilford, with Polignac's men taking potshots at me, puffs of dust erupting at my feet. I glanced back, saw them swabbing the cannon and dropping another pouch of gunpowder down the barrel. I picked up my pace.

Suddenly, there was sharp bugle reverie emanating from the far edge of the outer canyon, followed by a collective *huzzah* and the thundering of hooves and boots.

Colonel Connor and his dwindling regiment, numbering around seventy men, came charging at the Indian-garbed Rebs taking cover behind boulders. Two of the cannons were repositioned to aim at Union infantry, while the third was hitched to six horses and, three horse-mounted graybacks surrounding it, towed away from the escalating conflict. Meanwhile, the wagon that we'd believed was carrying Nellie and Emma began rolling.

The ground shook from the deafening roar of cannon fire. An explosion tore through Connor's ranks, iron cannonballs ripping through bodies and leaving gaping craters in its wake. Gripped by a desperate fury, the men in blue uniforms stepped forward, advancing steadily and closing the distance. Connor stood proudly on his white horse, saber raised in the air and shouting commands.

One of the horses, a draft that had been pulling the blown-up wagon, came trotting over, remnants of the harness dragging on the ground. I used my Bowie to cut loose the breeching and breast collar, grabbed the reins, and mounted the beast without a saddle by putting both hands on the hindquarters and boosting myself over and onto his back.

"Let's get Nellie and Emma," I said to him.

He took off after the wagon and Mormon cannon. I grabbed the horse's mane to avoid falling, which made things worse. Eventually, I found my balance, and soon I was close enough to draw my Colt from my holster. I considered shooting the horses but as we continued to gather speed, I saw a chance to plug the driver, who was frantically slapping the reins. As I drew nearer, I could hear his panicked shouts, voices carrying on the wind as he urged his horse to go faster.

My fingers steadied the Colt pistol as I took aim at the rear wheel of the wagon. There was too much jostling for me to bother sighting the gun.

My bullet found its mark, the wagon shuddering

violently as the wheel fractured into shards, causing the carriage to careen off course with a bone-jarring crash.

It was too much. Had I injured Nellie and Emma?

The cannon and six horses pulling it threaded an opening in the canyon walls and vanished.

As the dust settled, I trotted up to the wreckage, scanning the scene before me. There was no sign of the missing women. The driver lay sprawled on the ground, dazed and disoriented, his weapon lying several yards away in the sand. Unlike the others, he wore a Confederate uniform, and his leg was bent in the wrong direction.

I dismounted, my boots crunching on sunbaked earth as I approached the driver. He glared at me with hatred and defiance, knowing his time had run out. Night was falling, the sun expiring behind the mountains.

I pointed the Colt at him, drawing nearer as the light faded around us. "Where are they?"

He spat into the dust. "Straight to hell. Same place you're going, Yankee."

"I'm a Georgia boy," I said. "You sound like Arkansas."

"Little Rock. Ever been there?"

I nodded, still leveling the gun. "My native state is prettier."

The soldier winced as he tried to straighten his shattered limb. "Well, the *girls* certainly are. Prettier, too, than these belles you're chasing. I noticed you went for me and not the cannon."

"I don't like it when ugly men abduct the women around me. So, Reb, you wanna live?"

"Name's Foster. Sure. Who doesn't?"

"Tell me where they are, Foster."

I watched as he sized me up, and I helped his decision along by lowering the Colt. I knew what he was thinking; it was what *I'd* have thought in his position: If I don't tell him, I'm a dead man. I might be anyway, but if I do tell him, he might be a man of his word.

"They're with Captain Cajun," the Arkansas boy said. "Polignac is his name. He's a French duke."

"And where is *he*?" I cocked the hammer to let him know my patience was thinning.

"Inside the caves with Father Ephraim, the mad desert monk. I'd be careful, if I were you."

"Why is that?"

"He's not right. In his head, I mean. He's crazier than Captain Cajun. I'll bet the two of them are boiling those girls in a pot right now and fixing to eat 'em."

Did Foster really believe what he was saying? Father Ephraim a cannibal? I started feeling sorry for him. He could have been one of the boys I fought when we were young. Killing him would put him out of his broken-leg misery. Not killing him, he'd either die of thirst or Connor's troops would finish him off. And I'd have one less mortal soul on my conscience.

"I appreciate the information," I said, turning to leave. "Good luck to you, Foster. My name's Crimson, by the way."

"Th— Thanks, Kid," he said.

Gunfire cracked in the darkness, Connor's regiment and the Rebel platoon squeezing off their final shots before disengaging, nursing their wounds, and collecting their dead by starlight. I got back on the draft horse and slowly made my way through the opening in the canyon, through which the horses had pulled the cannon into Ephraim's dwelling.

My horse walked us through the wash, pebbles clacking under his hooves, until we reached a cave entrance, where a campfire was flickering. Entering the cavern, I could make out man sitting cross-legged, his back to us, face illuminated by the flames. There was no sign of the cannon, or the horses and men that had come through here. It was too dark for me to make out any tracks, and without a lantern or torch to light my way, I felt blind as a bat.

The shape of the man's head seemed familiar. I slid off the horse and drew my gun, slowly approaching the figure, his head down, resting on his chest.

The closer I got, the more I sensed something was wrong with him. Finally, I noticed that there was a blade sticking out of his chest, and as I stepped around him to view him in the firelight, I saw that it was Father Ephraim. He was dead, knife buried in his heart, just like Ustick.

Then I heard the click of a gun hammer behind me, and I raised my hands.

"*Pauvre vieux*," said the slithering European voice behind me, as he ripped the pistol from my grip. "The desert is an inhospitable place for old men. Don't you think, Kid?"

"Polignac," I said. "The French Confederate. What's your game."

"My game," he said, "is to cut off Lincoln's source of money. Before I do that, however, I'm going to make sure you don't annoy me again."

16

Inside a desert cave, gun pointed at my back, I watched shadows convulse on sandstone walls and waited for a bullet to shatter my spine. It never arrived. Instead, the fire crackled, licking hungrily at burning wood, orange sparks snapping and spinning upward into smoky darkness.

"Turn, Crimson," Polignac said, "and face your end."

Slowly, hands in the air, I about-faced. His uniform was crafted from wool and meticulously tailored, exuding authority and sophistication. His coat boasted gold braid embellishments that adorned the cuffs, collar, and front closure. Each button gleamed with polished brass, bearing the emblem of the Confederate States of America. Beneath the coat, he wore a crisp white shirt, collar fastened at the neck with a black silk cravat. The trousers, matching the coat in color and fabric, fit snugly over polished leather boots. Across the general's chest, a lavender sash was draped diagonally, and pinned to it was a gleaming brass buckle, engraved with the general's rank and unit insignia. He was taller and skinnier than

I'd expected, dripping elegance and charm in a smudged part of the world that made nobility impossible, unnecessary. The longer I studied his features, the more disgusted I grew. His chiseled jawline and piercing blue eyes reflected his aristocratic heritage. I could tell by examining him, by hearing his voice and smelling his cologne, that he'd led a life of privilege and influence, a life that should've been mine in another, kinder universe. Instead, my father was an industrious psychopath, rehearsing me to serve as his understudy in violence and annihilation.

Indeed, I felt like a stunted Telemachus encountering Thrasymedes—the polished, deadly warrior-son of King Nestor of Pylos—in the *Odyssey*.

"Your English is excellent," I said. "*Pour une grenouille.*"

He raised an eyebrow, smiled. "Ah, I see that you croak decent French for a Southerner. Too bad you're a traitor to your brothers, who fight with *me* against the forces of illegitimacy and decay."

"That *must* be why," I said, "so many of your kind ended up on a guillotine in the *Place de la Révolution*. Standing against illegitimacy and decay landed them there, no doubt."

Intrigued, he lowered his gun, but didn't holster it. "You're not the undisciplined savage you're made out to be in the dime novels, Kid. You speak French and know our history."

"My tutor was from Paris," I said, trying to buy more time. "He taught me chess, a game I hear you're pretty adept at."

The tension in Polignac's body drained a little, as if he perceived a kindred soul. "We simply *must* play a match before you die. You know, I'm curious, Kid. What happened to your tutor?"

I shrugged. "Last time I saw him he was packing medicinal lint into a bullet wound I'd given my father. We lost contact after that, I'm afraid."

"You're worse than a traitor," he sneered, holstering his gun, then removing his belt to toss it at a fellow Confederate whose presence I'd detected in the shadows. He rolled up his sleeves, smiling with malevolent pleasure, intending to clean my clock. "You're a coddled patricider."

The monster inside me was feverish, ready to snap its bonds. My voice went gravelly with murderlust as I took off my hat and bandolier, then my vest and shirt, letting them fall to the ground beside the fire, casting my shadow at great length across the cave floor. "I'll teach you a Latin-based word, frog. It's pronounced *decimation*."

"Show me, boy," he taunted. "Show me how you fight in Georgia."

I charged him, feinting with a lunge, then scrape-stomping the heel of my boot down his shin. He inhaled sharply through gritted teeth, then bull rushed me to thwart my temporary advantage. He was taller and had a longer reach, so I covered up, waiting for the moment that I might land a counterpunch. I'd engaged with Polignac head-on, toe to toe, thinking myself the more experienced pugilist. I'd been pit-fighting since I was nine years old, and it wasn't often that I squared up against someone who could best me in a dustup.

But it quickly dawned on me that Polignac had seriously studied the sport of boxing at a young age. I could discern this from the way he maintained a crouching stance, allowing him to shield his body and face while still allowing him to deliver powerful strikes. He never switched stances or changed position, challenging me to create unconventional angles. His shin was bleeding through his pants, but the injury didn't slow him in the slightest. He kept at me, hitting hard and covering up and using his weight to bully me into a defensive posture.

Beaten and bruised, the monster I'd unleashed grew angrier. So I got as low as I could, nearly squatting on my heels to duck under a punch, then tucking my head under his arm while grabbing him around the hamstring. I lifted with my legs, pushing my hips forward and using my arm over his shoulder to smash him to the dirt. He landed hard, but I made the mistake of following him to the ground instead of staying on my feet. He hook-gripped me with a side-choke that I couldn't escape, dragging my face against rocks, closer to the blazing fire.

I flipped over, trying to snag his back with my boot spurs and spoil his efforts to incinerate me, but he was too strong and soon I could smell my hair burning.

He growled into my ear, spittle-drenching me. "*Es une merde.*"

Desperate to avoid getting my nose seared off, I spotted my gun belt and used my legs to scoop it into the fire.

The Rebel that had joined Polignac inside the cave saw my ploy. "Sir, he kicked his ammo—"

He didn't finish. The belt had a few .75-caliber rounds packed with buckshot pellets, and they went off in a sharp series of explosions, giving me the distraction I needed to buck the French general and rabbit-punch him in the base of his skull.

He rolled before I could pin him, while his partner tried to bash me with the butt of his rifle. I was electrified with battle rage and wrestled the gun loose, bayoneting him in the crotch, then twisting the blade horrifically so that he bled from his femoral, splashing my hands with red gore. The soldier shrieked in terror as his life spilled out.

I yanked out the muzzle-blade, causing more blood to spurt, then thrust the weapon through the man's eye and into his brain, killing him instantly. He keeled over into the dust, which landed on the fire, sputtering the flames.

I jerked the bayonet again, then pivoted to swing it around and slice Polignac, but he was ready with a rock, smashing my cheek bone with such ferocity I thought he'd ruined my looks.

Stars blotted my vision as I clung to the rifle to avoid getting skewered. He cracked me again with the stone, and I was flat on my back, fingers numb and unable to hold the Enfield.

"Shame we won't get to play a chess match," he gloated above me as I waited for the death blow.

I heard him drop a musket ball into the barrel and ramrod it against powder and pin. The monster inside me screamed, urging me to get up and retaliate, but I was spent, battered, defeated by a Frenchman born with a silver spoon in his mouth and, apparently, boxing mitts in his crib.

I grabbed a handful of dust to throw in his eyes when I heard a familiar Irish cadence and saw a saber flash in the dwindling firelight, Polignac's rifle hacked into two pieces.

"I'll knock your pan in!" Colonel Connor said, sweaty and gunpowder-stained but otherwise bright-eyed and war-ripe.

He raised his sword, but the Frenchman parried the blow with the barrel half of the Enfield, then swoop-kicked the colonel, knocking him down. Connor didn't lose his saber though. From a prone position, he slashed at Polignac's feet, causing him to hurdle the blade like a skip rope.

Connor then sprung up and, blade pointed at Polignac, goosestep-marched directly at him, backing him up against the cavern wall.

Before the Irishman could pierce his target, the fire went out. We were plunged into darkness, with Connor's wild saber swings eliciting blue sparks as the metal impacted the sandstone.

"Hold still," Connor said, gasping for breath, "you cheese-eating frogger!"

Suddenly, there was light again, one of Connor's men entering the cavern with a torch. Polignac was nowhere to be seen. Concern all over his face, the soldier assessed his commander, no longer clumsily swatting the walls with a sword. The soldier then inspected me, finding a bruised, shirtless gunman brushing dust from his pants and wishing for a shot of whiskey. He drew the torch close to the dead Confederate, wincing when he spotted the terrible eye wound. Then he inspected Father Ephraim, making the sign of the cross when he realized the man was dead, too.

Feeling silly for not being able to so much as nick Polignac and realizing I was too exhausted to properly defend myself, Connor pounced, laying into me.

"Crimson," he said, returning his sword to its scabbard. "Once again, you've interfered in a highly sensitive military operation."

"I didn't anticipate you'd engage the enemy at this juncture, sir," I said, struggling to stand. "But I appreciate your rescue. The Frenchman was getting the upper hand before you arrived."

Satisfied with my gratitude, Connor used his fingers to smooth the pipes of his horseshoe mustache. Then he seemed to believe he should remain mad and squinted. There was a tension between us, the crackling of the soldier's torch and our breathing the only noises in the cave. The soldier, I remembered his name as Gallagher, ignited a juniper branch to hand me.

Finally, Connor said, "It *does* appear that you located the Mormon gunsmith at Goblin. President Lincoln will appreciate your efforts in helping us ship these weapons to the Union."

I nodded wearily. Feeling like I might puke, I paused before replying. "Rocker Portwell and his foundrymen were attacked by Polignac. Three cannons were stolen. We recovered two, but one is missing. The Frenchman confessed his conspiracy to destroy silver mining in Virginia City."

Connor's eyes clouded with regret. "I lost more than a few men to Polignac's recruitment efforts. Our cook ended up a disappointment, poisoning us with undercooked pork and hurting morale."

I recalled that it was Poppy's uncle John John who'd sold a tapeworm-infected hog to Connor's regiment. I decided to keep this information to myself. "We should intercept and kill Polignac," I said, "before he tows the cannon to Virginia City. With that weapon, he can severely damage mining operations. He's in the canyon somewhere."

Outside, there was a whoop, followed by the stamping of horse's hooves and rifle fire.

"It seems," Connor said, "that we're under attack again."

"Wait, those can't be Polignac's men still impersonating the Ute."

"I imagine it's the *real* Indians."

"Come on now, what?"

"The ones whose camp we burned earlier today."

I resisted the urge to pinch the bridge of my nose. Connor was now in a running gun battle with Paiute and French Confederates. "Polignac didn't just steal a cannon," I explained. "He kidnapped two of my friends."

Connor shook his head in disdain over the enemy's actions. "I can't spare you any men. Thus, I hereby give you the authority to track the frogger on your own, Kid."

I shook the colonel's hand. "Thanks for your help, sir. I won't let you down."

"Good luck, Kid. Let's move, Gallagher."

As they headed toward the fray, I donned my hat, put on my shirt and coat and bandolier, raised my torch, and pushed deeper into the cave, looking for a familiar landmark. For a moment, I thought I might be lost, as turn after turn seemed to take me further away from points of reference. But then I saw the beaver-shaped boulder, and when I took the path on the left it led me into the cavern that had been filled with shimmering gold.

Alas, the glitter was gone, the cavern standing empty and forlorn. The treasure had been snatched, and Father Ephraim murdered. Contemplating what had happened here made me sick.

I spotted a single gold coin on the floor and pocketed it.

Polignac didn't just steal a Mormon cannon and two beautiful women whose company I happened to enjoy. He had millions in precious metal to use in his campaign to wipe Virginia City off the map of the Western United States.

I had a completely new reason to kill the bastard before he capped his evil plan.

17

Time lost its meaning in the caves. A minute stretched into an hour as I tracked Polignac's bootprints by torchlight through sinuous corridors, each seemingly identical yet subtly distinct from the last. Sandstone walls whispered secrets of eons past, lost voices of humanity murmuring in darkness. A waterfall splashed like a celestial dream. Was it all a mirage curling at the edges of my pain-racked mind? I didn't think so. It felt like the fulfillment of a wish, to be banished below the surface, hidden from the insanity of humankind, safely interred.

As I threaded my way to the mouth of the cave on the canyon's opposite end, I carried humility in my heart. In Graves Valley, I'd witnessed nature's raw power, its amaranthine beauty, even while nearly dying at the hands of a diabolical Frenchman. Buried deep within the guts of the earth, I felt somehow closer to God's baleful eye, recognizing the cold justice in His judgment. He perceived me in the subterranean depths, still cared about me despite the bad choices I'd accumulated. I had one decision left, of course. I'd choose to leave Virginia City and become a citrus farmer. Or I'd stay and die senselessly in a pile of mining refuse while upholding order in a town of madness and depravity. Or I'd wait for whatever Poppy might have in the back of her mind for us to do after making enough of a fortune and feeding the addictions of enough opium smokers. If I could convince Poppy to join me in California, my life wouldn't be in vain. Instead, I'd be forgiven for sending so many souls to hell—forgiven, that is, by the highest power in a sinless realm, where my father's influence held no sway.

Or maybe I was simply delusional from exhaustion and getting my head pounded by a rock.

In any case, I heard footsteps creeping up behind me as I drew closer to the cave exit, visible now as sunrise blossomed. Polignac's tracks, too, were evident. I clung to the shadowy edges of the wall until I was outside, then climbed up above the mouth of the cavern, gazing down to see who had followed me. I had no pistol or gun belt, having lost them in my fracas with Polignac. Hopefully whoever emerged had a weapon for me to use after I dispatched him.

I heard three voices. As I raised a boulder to skull-crush one of them, I identified the men—Rocker Portwell and Elders Wilford and Spencer.

"To see, once more, the stars," I said to them, quoting the last book in Dante's *Inferno*.

They looked up at me, smiling brightly in spite of how badly it had gone once Polignac directed the cannons at us. "That from a godless poem, Kid?" Rocker said.

"The most god-*full* verse, actually," I said, scampering down the cliff to greet them. "The three of you escaped

Polignac, Connor's cavalry charge, and a real Indian attack."

They retained their happy grins, with Elder Wilford being the first to embrace me.

"Ever clasped arms with a gentile before?" I said.

"Never," Elder Spencer said, leaning in. "We'll make an exception for you, Kid."

Even a grumpy Rocker stepped forward to slap my back affectionately. "Sure, your scheme to rescue Nellie and Emma almost got us killed, but here we are in the morning sun, still alive and kicking. And if I'm honest about it, Kid, I had a pretty good time."

"Shame about the Gatling gun, though," I said. "I was just starting to get good with it."

We set out in the hope of locating a fading outlaw trail that my Paiute pal Snake had mentioned the last time I saw him in Virginia City. I wasn't exactly sure that it stretched this far east, but since he knew everything about obscure roosts and hideouts, I figured there was a decent chance we'd find it.

Elder Wilford looked at the sun as it continued to scale the cloudless blue firmament. "We have no horses. No weapons. How do we catch Polignac? And if we somehow do, how do we fight?"

At that moment, we heard the clatter and creak of a covered wagon pulled by four draft horses, approaching from around an elevated cluster of Russian thistle and Indian ricegrass. On the tall, billowing white tarp, a colorful bodiless arm with a bulging bicep flexed above the words: DOKTOR SKORPION STRENGTH SERUM. In the driver's seat, a short, mustachioed man wearing a striped top hat and a fancy striped suit held the reins, singing a tune that I recognized as "Oh, Boys, Carry Me 'Long."

"I know this fellow," I said to Rocker, recalling an incident last year when, returning to Virginia City from Rattlepeak, Sarah had kidnapped Skorpion's three-legged dog.

The Mormons looked at me, then at one another, trying to figure how we intended to play this.

The wagon hadn't made it all the way around the bend when I motioned to Rocker and Wilford to seek cover and instructed Elder Spencer to lie down on the ground. He sat down, keeping his back straight, until I urged him to lie flat.

I walked up to Skorpion's wagon, waving my arms in a plea for him to stop the cart. No longer carrying a tune, he pulled on the reins with one hand, raised his scattergun with the other.

"Young man," he said. "I'm not hospitable to bandits, so if you'll kindly remove yourself and your pretending-to-be-ill pal from my path, we won't need to endure unnecessary conflict."

"My friend can't move," I said, arms raised, Rocker and Wilford hiding behind a boulder in my peripheral vision. "He's stricken with palsy. Might you offer a remedy for gold?" I pulled from my pocket the coin that I'd found in Father Ephraim's cave and showed it to Skorpion.

His eyes grew big. "Why, yes! I have just the strength serum to cure your young friend."

Still holding his gun, Skorpion, awkwardly plump, stepped off the buckboard and went around to the back of his wagon to fetch a bottle of snake oil. I turned to look at Rocker and Wilford, obscured behind rock, each of them now carrying branches, ready to wallop the salesman. I gave them a nod, letting them know it was almost time to tee up.

Skorpion latched the wagon's tailgate and walked over with a bottle of magic serum. I handed him the coin, which he bit theatrically and, pleased, emitted an eerie leprechaun giggle. "Tastes like real gold." He gave me the bottle, which I held at a distance from me like a dead cat.

"I'm afraid I can't give it to him," I said.

Skorpion had just turned back to his horses. "Why not?"

"I don't believe in snake oil."

"Unfair, sir!" he said, incensed and defensive, stomping toward me to peer into my face. "Dr. Skorpion is, I'll have you know, thoroughly licensed and registered in the territories of Nevada, Utah, and Colorado. This isn't the oil of any serpent, young man. What you hold in your hands is thoroughly and genuinely a proprietary, trademark-filed elixir. All you need to do is partake of a single swallow from that bottle comprising a blend of soothing herbs and healing Seneca oil, extracted from the rarest glands of the powerful croco-dragons in the mystical reaches of Bolivia—animals that live for five hundred years!"

"I've read about the croco-dragons," I said. "In *Atlantic Monthly*, I think."

"Undoubtedly. The name Skorpion is known from the mining camps of the west to the stock markets of the east. Here, now, let me show you how to apply it to your friend."

Spencer inhabited his role with startling zeal, feigning muscle spasms.

"Oh dear," I said. "It's too late."

"Nonsense," Skorpion said, taking the bottle from me and uncorking it. "Hold him still."

I pressed down on Spencer's chest, pinning him to

the spot as the quack doctor dribbled elixir onto the Mormon's face.

"Blegh!" Spencer gagged, sitting up and using his shirt to wipe his mouth.

"It's a miracle!" I exclaimed. "He's cured!"

"Judging by his raiment, I'd say his ailment isn't palsy," Skorpion said, inspecting Spencer's clothing, specifically his leaf-green linen trousers. "He seems exhausted by plural marriage."

"Don't be rude," Rocker growled, towering behind him, along with Wilford.

Skorpion whimpered and attempted to swing the barrel of his gun at the voice. But Rocker was too fast, ripping the weapon from the stocky man's grip. Then he pointed it at the quack.

"We need weapons, Skorpion," Wilford said. "What's in the wagon?"

"I have— well, *lots* of things." He seemed deflated, woefully resigned to being robbed by Mormons and their bandit accomplice.

"Show us," Spencer said.

Arms up, Skorpion led us to the rear of the wagon, pausing before he opened the latch.

Rocker nudged him with the scattergun. "Let's see it."

"I'm—I'm too frightened," Skorpion said. "My hands are shaking."

Rocker sighed in disgust and, in one a swift motion, unlatched the tailgate and pulled back the canvas flap, expecting to find unsold bottles of strength serum. Instead, his eyes widened in disbelief as he beheld the hungry gaze of a lion glaring at him from behind the iron bars of a cage. The smell was revolting.

The world around us seemed to stand still as Rocker

and the animal locked eyes, both frozen in a moment of primal instinct.

"That's the lion," I said, "from Circus Southwest."

The creature's growl rumbled like distant thunder, muscles coiled and ready to pounce. My heart raced in his chest as I realized that Skorpion had no idea how to care for a lion. The animal likely hadn't eaten in several days.

Suddenly, the beast lunged forward, its huge jaws clanging the bars of the cage, gusting us with putrescent halitosis. Every one of us jumped back.

"Skorpion," I said. "Why the heck are you traveling across Utah with an escaped lion?"

"I—I figured I could sell it when I reached Salt Lake."

"What can the Mormons do with a lion?" Wilford said, rubbing his mouth in disbelief.

I noticed picked-clean bones in the cage. "Tell me those aren't human."

"I used a rotten mule deer carcass to lure him into the cage. When the Ute attacked the circus, the lion tamer set him free."

"Emma needs rescuing," Spencer reminded huffily. "Let's kill him and drive to Virginia City."

"N—no, please," Skorpion begged. "Take my wagon and spare me."

"He didn't mean killing *you*," I said. "He was referring to the lion."

"No, I meant Skorpion," Spencer said with a wink. The Mormon boys had loosened up.

Even Rocker was smiling. "How do we remove the lion from the wagon without getting eaten?"

"We're keeping this beautiful creature," I said. "He's the new mascot of Virginia City. Sarah will adore him."

Wilford's response was priceless. "Women in your town appreciate this kind of…gift?"

"You have no idea," I said, "about the women in my town."

They grinned, not knowing how to respond. Then we all frowned, recalling the current fate of Nellie and Emma, who needed rescuing. Finally, Rocker said, "This area is swarming with jackrabbits. I'll snare a few for us and the lion."

"I prefer mine cooked," Wilford said, "if that's okay with everyone."

"This gun all you have as far as weapons?" I asked Skorpion.

"I—I have a tube," he said. "With a rocket in it."

Wilford peered into the wagon, flinching when the lion shifted in his cage. "How's that?"

I knew what Skorpion was trying to describe. It was a Hale rocket launcher, a metal tube that fired seven-inch-long rockets more than 2,000 yards. Accuracy was terrible, but the rockets, typically filled with black gunpowder, generated an awful lot of noise and chaos. I'd only heard of the US Navy deploying this weapon, using it against Confederates.

"Where'd you get it?"

"A soldier in the Union regiment gave it to me in exchange for Ute jewelry and clothes."

"Ustick," I said. "The bastard. But at least we have *some* kind of weapon. Skorpion, cover that cage with blankets so I can fish around for the tube. Rocker, let's have you working on that jackrabbit stew. I'm so hungry my stomach believes my throat's been slit."

"Kid," Rocker said. "I hate to say it, but we should move in the direction of Virginia City, since that's where Polignac is ultimately headed. Maybe we can rescue

Nellie and Emma before the French Rebs strikes. The four of us are battered and need to heal."

Elders Wilford and Spencer didn't look happy about it, but they nodded wearily in agreement. It was true that we looked like hammered burro scat. Rocker's knife wounds were still healing, and I didn't feel well at all after my tussle with Polignac.

"Okay, but we should stop in Silver Reef," I said. "We might get a tip on Polignac's location."

"You're taking me with you?" Skorpion said. "To Virginia City?"

"Yes," I said. "The men will require your elixirs to fuel their mine operations."

"I'd have visited before, but the bandits that surround Mount Ophir are notorious."

"We may encounter a few highwaymen."

"That doesn't sound promising. Will we make it?"

"Maybe not to heaven, given the starving lion and the rocket launcher. But we'll definitely reach Virginia City."

18

We made sure to feed the lion first, calming him down enough so that we could investigate everything Skorpion had tucked into his wagon. Rocker's roasted jackrabbit was delicious, seasoned with salt and spices that the traveling snake oiler had brought with him. Bone-tired from our skirmishes with Polignac, we watered the horses before lighting out for Virginia City, planning a detour to Silver Reef to send a telegram to Ralston and perhaps buy two more horses for our wagon, borrowing the gold coin, and some others, from Skorpion that I promised to pay back with interest when we got home to the Comstock. I felt confident that, if we stayed on the outlaw trail, we could beat the Confederates to Nevada, but only if we avoided ambush and injuries.

It was a day's ride to Silver Reef and when we arrived the shops along the main thoroughfare were shuttering even as the saloons began to fill with rowdy miners and riffraff. We parked the wagon behind an abandoned tannery near the town creek and left Spencer and Skorpion there to watch the lion. Wilford, Rocker, and I walked the horses over to the livery and paid for the animals to be washed, and for the farrier to reset their shoes. I also bought two more horses before sending a Western Union missive to Ralston:

```
FOUND STEELWORKS
ONE NAPOLEON GUN MISSING
PURSUING FRENCH REBS TO VC
GULLY WASHER IMMINENT
KC
```

"Going into town tonight, Kid?" Wilford asked.

"Rocker and I are conducting reconnaissance."

"Reconnaissance, Elder Portwell? I hope that's not a fancy term for drinking."

Rocker chuckled. "I'm backing up Crimson while he pursues an investigation."

Wilford yawned. "Well, I'm sunburned and road-wrecked. I'm going to curl up next to the big stinking kitty and get some shuteye."

Rocker and I headed in the direction of the saloon, where I'd chatted with Polignac's favorite lady of the night, Winifred. I didn't need to share my intentions with the Mormon enforcer. He was shrewd and cunning and would've suggested the idea himself. I found that I often had a strange and compelling bond with hardened killers and madmen. It's not that we understood one another—who, after all, could ever hope to fathom the savage mentality of Kid Crimson—but that we both viewed the calculus of violence as the ultimate system of reasoning. We were advanced practitioners who never tired of solving the equation and applying it to every situation.

"Holy Moses, I assume?" Rocker said.

"I can't think of a better establishment in *this* town." More of Skorpion's money jangled in my pocket.

"Might be better if we rested. Currently, we resemble the rear end of a stomped opossum."

"I've looked and smelled worse. Besides, I plan on Winifred giving me a little scrub tonight."

Rocker laughed. "She'll give you more than a bath. Maybe you should give me Skorpion's purse, Kid."

"Sure, Rocker." To his surprise, I gave it all to him. "Buy me a whiskey at least."

He put the money in his coat. "Never ordered a drink, but I'll do my best."

"That why they called you Peter Priesthood last time? You subscribe to a higher morality?"

"I don't drink," Rocker growled, "because it throws my aim when I'm killing gentile governors."

I didn't have a comeback for that one. I smiled and pushed open the batwing doors of the Holy Moses.

The place was fully gassed and set to burn. The men drank and gambled boisterously, with the piano player pounding the keys with sweaty abandon. Three bartenders were dashing around to keep up with the dozens of customers circulating at the mahogany bar. Coins seemed to flash everywhere—on poker tables, into the hands of soiled doves, tossed into the air for waiters to catch—and it occurred to me that, if it wasn't for the excruciating overhead, I could probably do worse than manage a bar in a streak-happy mining town full of people with poor impulse control. Maybe Poppy would join me in the endeavor. Then again, I was as much a victim of my own dark whims as anyone. Unlike most people, I could name my demons and refused to make excuses for the ease with which they seduced me.

There were no open tables. As Rocker and I bellied up to the bar, I sensed a female presence drawing near. I let her approach, and soon she reached out to gently grab my arm. "Kid Crimson. Remember me?"

I turned slowly to give her my steady gaze, but I'm sure she noticed my mouth fall open. The shiner on her face was far worse than mine, glistening and multi-colored.

"Or rather," she continued, looking at the floor, "do you *recognize* me? I...I fell into a spell of bad luck."

I carefully placed my fingers under her chin so I could look into her eyes. "Winnie, who did it?"

"Kid, I'm fine. Really, it doesn't hurt."

"It was the French Rebel," I said. "The man you mentioned when I saw you last."

She redirected my question. "Is that why you left so abruptly? I thought that might've been the reason. I didn't want to think...well, that you didn't *want* me."

Before I could answer, Rocker approached with two glasses of beer. I took them from him, giving one to Winnie.

"Ma'am," he said, doffing his hat. "Name's Rocker. Wonderful to meet you."

"You can call me Winnie," she said. "I—I don't mean to take your beer, Mr. Rocker. I can get my own—"

"Oh no, Miss Winnie," he interrupted smoothly. "I don't drink. I'm here to support my friend Crimson, who is a passionate inebriate."

I laughed. "Rocker, I drink more, I imagine, than your entire church."

"You don't have to imagine, Kid."

This made Winnie snort. "You two are a funny couple."

"We've been through a lot together," I said.

Rocker nodded, then said to us, "Beg pardon, but I need fresh air. The cigarette smoke has aggravated my humors. Kid, I ordered a dozen steaks for our friends. Should I save you one?"

"No thanks, Rocker. I plan to dine later."

"A dozen steaks?" Winnie's eyebrows shot up. "You have hungry friends."

"That we do. Until next time, Miss Winnie."

"Thank you for the beer, Rocker!"

I watched her take a dainty sip and felt her grip on my bicep tighten. Then she rested her head against my chest, the two of us standing just outside a cluster of animated poker games.

"Winnie, darling."

"Yes, Kid?"

"I reek like a lion cage on fire."

She pressed her nose to my shoulder and inhaled. "I think you smell delicious."

"Do you have access to hot water and soap?"

"Kid Crimson," she said, voice tinged with offense. "Silver Reef is a civilized location."

"I'm sure, darling. Can you civilize *me* with a hot bath?"

"Oh yes. I can do that—and more."

IN HER ROOM above the Holy Moses, Winnie stripped to her corset and drawers before pouring several buckets of coal-heated water, nearly boiling, into a spacious, claw-footed porcelain tub she claimed had been shipped from Paris. Then she dumped a box of lemon-scented soap flakes into the water, creating a bubbly expanse into which I soaked my worn, abraded body.

The rest of the experience was life-changing. I'd never been so thoroughly scrubbed, Winnie wielding a pink cotton washcloth with true virtuosity. She brushed my armpits, my butt crack, and in between my toes, leaving me in a blissful state of anticipation, stimulation. Her bed looked freshly laundered and inviting. We could still hear the noise of the saloon below, but I also felt our hearts beating here in this perfumed den of sensuality and romance.

When I thought about my Mormon brothers and the snake oiler sleeping beside a rancid lion on the hard ground, I laughed out loud.

"You seem," she said, bringing her lips close to mine, "to be really enjoying your bath, Kid."

I reached for her soft blondeness, undoing her chignon and wrapping her locks in my loose fist. I kissed her mouth, which didn't reek of alcohol. This time she tasted like marshmallow icing on a Lady Baltimore cake. I wanted to pull her into the tub and devour her neck with bubbles in her hair. Despite her injured face, she radiated loveliness. I kissed her again, mindful of her bruises.

In response to a knock, she stood up and left the room, closing the door behind her. She returned a few moments later, carrying a silver serving tray with a plated steak and boiled potato and what looked like a cup of black coffee.

"Your dinner has arrived," she said, placing the tray on a stand next to the tub. "You should eat a steak...and then I'll eat you."

Again, there was a knock. "Oh my, what else did I order!"

She went back into the living room to answer, again closing the door. As I reached over to begin knifing the piping-hot ribeye, I heard a commotion, the sound of Winnie's yelp as she was shoved against furniture, followed by the clumping of boots and, in a furious spasm of violence, the door was kicked off its hinges, splinters flying.

Polignac, still in his uniform, stood before me, raising a .44-caliber single-shot Derringer.

"Checkmate," he announced, squeezing the trigger.

In one fluid motion, I yanked the serving tray, using it as a shield to deflect the bullet, which ricocheted and shattered Winnie's dressing mirror.

In the process, I sent my food and coffee flying at Polignac, splattering and burning him.

Incensed, he grabbed one of Winnie's hairpins and slashed, but I was standing and again swung the tray in time to block his thrust, causing a teeth-aching screech of metal scratching metal.

My hands were still wet, but I managed to twist the hairpin from his grip and backhand him into the window curtains.

Glass on the floor sliced my feet as I made my way toward him, determined to end his life.

"You made a mistake coming here." I gasped.

"I don't think so," Polignac replied, reaching up to wrench the brass curtain rod. "What is the sport that is becoming so popular now in the United States? Baseball, I believe it's called."

I charged him with the hairpin, but I miscalculated the length of the curtain rod as it crashed against my chin. The impact was devastating.

I found myself crawling on my hands and knees, to where I didn't know, when I heard Polignac taunting me.

"Every traitor deserves to die this way," he said. "Naked and afraid."

He grabbed me by the hair and I felt the prick of the hairpin against my neck.

Suddenly, Winnie stormed into her bedroom, screaming as she fired her own pistol at Polignac, grazing his shoulder.

"*Putain*," he said, before jumping out the window.

I started to lose consciousness. The sum total of the beatings, hardships, and exhaustion overwhelmed me and I felt myself slipping away.

"Thanks for the scrub, Winnie. Sorry I didn't kill that lunatic."

"Kid," she said, the look of fear on her face revealing that this might be my final moment. "I don't think Camile Polignac is your cousin. Where are your friends staying?"

My jaw ached and I could barely get the words out, but the fact that I could speak meant my mandible wasn't broken. "They're sleeping. Next to a covered wagon. Full of snake oil. Mormons. Behind the old tannery."

"I'll send someone to fetch Rocker. And I'll summon the doctor, if he's not pass-out drunk."

"Winnie," I said. "I need to tell you something important."

"You have a beautiful Chinese girlfriend in Virginia City. I know, Kid. I read the entire dime novel front to back."

"No," I said. "There's a circus lion in the wagon. Don't let anyone hurt him."

"A lion? Why would anyone hurt such a majestic creature."

"My mother."

"What?"

"She was majestic and my father killed her."

I yearned to tell her the whole sad saga, but oblivion found me.

19

Nightmares swallowed me, hideous images of my father's Georgia plantation coruscating in my mind as I tossed and turned, sweating for two days in the back of a bumpy wagon that Rocker and Winnie drove to Virginia City. Memories of a miserable childhood transformed into dire visions of my savage antics in a mining town plagued by grotesque trolls disemboweling the earth for gleaming riches, eviscerating every mountain in search of grubby minerals, a vampire's fanged mouth dripping blood-colored mercury with the fire of madness burning in his pupil-stripped eyes as darkness covered the West, while the other monsters coyote-yipped their wretched desires at a pale moon. Tapered snouts and black noses pointed toward malevolent starlight as a shroud of soul-lashing insanity fog-blanketed the peaks and valleys in God's country, desperate neighs of wild mustangs echoed through canyons, reverberating along with the mobile shooting gallery of railway passengers armed with rifles in boxcars overflowing with bullet casings. Visions of bright-red gore splattering acacia and

Joshua trees as morbid vultures pinwheeled in a cloud-smeared sky the color of a peach, until it evolved into iridescent hues of a woman's bruised face, and I saw Nellie on her knees in the dusty foothills with Polignac holding a blade to her neck and laughing maniacally as I raced to her aid, only to arrive too late.

A scream.

Torrent of blood.

Cannon blasting the town from Mount Ophir.

Poppy's opium den pulverized.

Verbena's Blood Nugget obliterated.

Ezra and Sarah in the dust like forgotten ragdolls.

My mother's casket lowered into the ground in the Boot Hill cemetery.

My black lover Hanna hung from a noose outside the opera house as Chaparral played "Deus Irae" on a piano.

When I came to, I was lying in my favorite coffin in Grover's funeral home in Virginia City, dressed in my pajamas with the morning sun streaming through the bay windows, the smell of formaldehyde and wood shavings in the air. I sat up slowly, touching my jaw which ached only slightly. I ran my tongue along my teeth; to my surprise, I hadn't lost any from Polignac's concussive baseball swing, a small miracle. I scanned the casket room and saw my gorgeous Poppy barely sitting in a battered saloon chair, her lithe body slumped from the fatigue of watching over me all night, her gorgeous, raven-black hair undone and almost touching the floor. She wore a tight-fitting orange *qipao* dress with a standing collar and pearl-bead knot buttons and yellow floral-embroidered mesh slippers, and in that moment, I had to stifle a sob brought on by the sight of her, her breathtaking appearance amid the containers of the deceased.

I tried to speak, but there was no sound. I rubbed my throat and coughed.

Poppy shot up and joined me at my coffin, resting on a marble display stand. She leaned forward to kiss my forehead, keeping her hair from falling into my face. She smelled like agave oil, and I couldn't believe how fortunate I was to have a woman so strong and loving as Poppy.

"How long?" I croaked out like a desiccated frog.

"Three days. You got here the night before last in one of two wagons. Seems you have new friends, Kid."

"I do?"

She crossed her arms, taking a step back. "Mormons, a runaway circus lion, and a whore."

"That *does* sound like the company I tend to keep, yes." Now I sounded like the front end of Rocker's stomped opossum.

"Did you sleep with her?"

"It's a *male* lion, Poppy."

"After nearly dying, you can't stop making light."

"I didn't sleep with her. Did Ralston ask about me?"

She nodded. "He's eager to chat. So is this Rocker fellow. Ralston has been talking with him and seems very interested in the Mormon cannon foundry."

I was about to ask if she knew anything about Polignac and his Rebels when Grover showed up.

"Back from the dead," he said, handing me a coffee. "Kid, I envy your recovery skills."

With Poppy's assistance, I carefully stepped out of my coffin, took a sip, and immediately felt better. "There's no skill involved. Just dumb luck. How are Ezra and Sarah?" The coffee lubricated my larynx and I almost sounded normal to myself.

"Oh, they're having a blast with their new pet. No

one could understand why you dragged a lion to Virginia City."

I started to laugh, but my jaw throbbed so I stopped. "Seriously? That girl is supernatural."

Grover shrugged. "Well, she *is* taking lessons from Ringmaster Clyde. The poor fellow barely survived an Indian attack. Circus Southwest was ambushed, and they tried to scalp him, gashing him pretty darn good. He made it back here on foot. I stitched him up best I could. They've been working with Chaparral on a new show for the opera house stage."

"Would it surprise you," I said, "to know it wasn't Indians that attacked Circus Southwest?"

Grover shook his head. "Clyde described the raid rather oddly. Doesn't sound like an Indian attack."

"French Confederates, along with traitors from Colonel Connor's regiment, led by Prince Polignac."

"Interesting. You might want to see Rosie when your strength returns. She saw something in that seer stone she uses to make money. Something disturbing...you know, I'll let *her* explain."

"Grover," I said. "You're a Christian. You can't believe in Rosie's Jack Mormon palmistry."

"Outside of the Bible," he said, "there's nothing else for *me*. After all, I'm a man surrounded by death. Other people, though...well, they might have different strategies."

"Polignac's strategy is to obliterate Virginia City with a cannon."

"None of the French Rebs, and none of Connor's Union boys, have visited the Sure Cure," Poppy said. "My cousin Sing and I are watching out for them."

"I don't even know," I said, "if Connor and his men

are alive. They ended up being attacked by *real* Indians after mixing it up with Polignac's platoon."

Grover picked up a hammer from a workbench to tap a nail that had been jutting out slightly on my casket. "I'm sure I don't need to tell you, Kid, that Virginia City doesn't have anything that can stand up to a cannon."

"I realize that. But I have a plan for improving our odds."

Grover smiled. "You always do, Kid."

Suddenly, Ezra rushed into the room, saw me, and gave me a crashing hug. "Kid! You're alive!"

"Oof, yes, you can't kill a Crimson so easily. I swear you've grown since I saw you last."

"It's all the food Poppy feeds me," Ezra said. "If I want to be a gunfighter like you, I need to be tall and strong."

Poppy glared at me. Grover almost said something, but instead tapped a few more nails.

"Ezra," I said. "You're too smart and clever to be a hired gun. Don't you want to be rich?"

He thought about this. "Like Ralston, you mean."

I nodded. "Yes, I mean he practically owns this town."

"Aww, he's boring and heavyset, Kid. All he carries is a Derringer. That's a woman's gun."

Poppy playfully slapped his neck. "Women can kill, too, you know!"

But the word "Derringer" had scabbed my mind as I recalled the repulsive memory of Polignac shooting at me.

"Kid, you okay?"

"I'm fine, Poppy. Really."

"Speaking of Ralston," Ezra said. "He told me to stir

you and then drag you to the Griddle of Doom for pancakes."

"Tell him I'll be there in an hour. I need a bath first."

"You can count on me! Oh, and is it true what the traveling salesman says?"

"Skorpion? What did he tell you?"

"That you stole his dog last year. And *this* year you robbed him of a lion."

"It's true," I said. "I didn't do it intentionally. Unexpected things happen on the trail when you're on assignment."

"That's what I worry about," Poppy said.

RALSTON WAS ALREADY SEATED in the corner booth. When I joined him, the server brought us two plates of delicious cinnamon pancakes and two black coffees. The sight and smell of this meal reinvigorated my senses. Ralston appeared unruffled as always, smiling as he inspected his silverware. Satisfied with its spotlessness, he tucked into his breakfast.

"Sorry, but I couldn't wait," he said. "My hunger gets the better of me in stressful times."

"You seem placid, actually. How was Virginia City in my absence?" Starving, I shoved a piece of flapjack into my maw despite the soreness of chewing.

"On the whole? Definitely rowdier. I know Verbena would prefer to have you watching over her establishments. But Chaparral and Jericho did a fine job suppressing the rabble."

"Only the circus was attacked outside the town limits?"

He shook his head, swallowing coffee to wash down

his pancake. "We lost a departing Wells Fargo stagecoach and, more troubling, an incoming carriage of gunpowder."

"For the mines."

"Sure, but you're aware, of course, of gunpowder's other uses."

I couldn't believe what I was hearing. "Cannon fire. Ralston, I regret losing that gun. Polignac has it, and he'll use it. I have no doubt about that."

Ralston momentarily raised himself from his seat to affectionately pat my shoulder. "Don't be hard on yourself. You were on a scouting mission. You ended up minimizing what could've been an apocalyptic scenario. The Mormons came close to losing *all* their cannons at Goblin Valley."

"Rocker told you?"

"He did, but he shouldn't worry. I placed a huge amount of money into an account in Zion's Savings Bank and Trust Company for the guns, which are being shipped east as we chew pancakes. I told him you had negotiated with the president. Still, Rocker is concerned that losing a cannon will cause Lincoln to subjugate his church."

"Will it?"

Ralston scoffed. "The order of annihilation goes like you imagine it does—Rebs. Indians. Blacks. Mormons."

"Blacks?" I suddenly lost my appetite, clattering my fork on the table. "Your sense of comedy is rotten, Ralston."

He shrugged and popped more pancake into his jowly mouth. "The United States is a white Christian nation, Kid. Mormons aren't exactly Christian, but neither are they completely hostile to our religious principles, outside of forbidding adultery and incest, naturally."

Feeling my face redden, I wiped my mouth with a napkin. "Let's refocus on the task at hand. How do you suggest I track down Polignac before he shoots twelve-pound cannonballs into a mining town covered in gunpowder?"

"He'll get here when he's good and ready. He now has a lot of gold that he needs to exchange for French mercenaries and French cannons."

I couldn't help but remove my hat and tug on my hair in dismay. "He's bringing *more* guns here? With Father Ephraim's cave treasure, I bet."

"That wasn't Ephraim's gold. Ephraim was a lunatic and a borderline cannibal who cooked and ate bandits who stayed in his lair. It was a secret bank the US was allowing him to operate so that we could build guns to smash the Texas Confederacy and the Knights of the Golden Circle."

I noticed that what the Arkansas soldier Foster had said about Ephraim was true. "Pinch them from the West. Sure, but you can't be serious about France helping Polignac to such a degree."

"He's aristocracy, the crème of the nobility. They'd do anything for him, including allow him to travel to the Southern United States to fight with the Confederacy. He's won three battles for them, yet the war still grinds in favor of the Union. This is Polignac's chance to deliver a knockout blow by cutting off Lincoln's money. No silver, no weapons."

"I'm learning," I said, "many things this morning that I wish I didn't know."

"There was a reason God told Adam and Eve to never partake of fruit from the knowledge tree."

"God made things he had no business making," I said. "My father, for instance."

Having finished his meal, he signaled the server for a coffee refill. "Speaking of members of the Golden Circle, I hear you took Nellie Brown with you to Utah."

"Yes. Nellie is as lethal as she is altruistic. She was instrumental in helping me safeguard a girl, Dolly, after her family was slaughtered by Polignac. Dolly's with the Mormons now. As for Nellie—"

"We know where Nellie is, Kid," Ralston cut me off, making a sour face while pushing something across the table. "But do you know where she's been?"

It was a wedding daguerreotype of Nellie, smiling and looking beautiful in a white lace dress. Beside her was the dapper groom in a black officer's uniform, an arrogant militarist, someone I didn't expect to see standing next to a woman I cherished and believed beyond reproach.

The man was Polignac.

20

STUNNED BY WHAT RALSTON HAD REVEALED, I headed to Rosie's apartment, where I hoped to find her and Chaparral. They were usually awake at this hour, Chaparral tinkering on a spinet, polishing an original composition before leaving for the opera house. He enjoyed playing his music on a grand piano, projecting it into an acoustically pristine space, one that was visually splendid, full of glass-windowed grandeur and sunlight. The owner, Myles Dominick, recognized Chap's tune-smithing, investing, to a small degree, in a promising young saloon musician who might very well write the next *Po-ca-hon-tas: The Gentle Savage*. Myself, I loathed musicals and found comedies abhorrent. In truth, I rarely enjoyed a clownish stage show, preferring refined touring productions of opera and ballet, which my mother introduced me to in Atlanta when I was a child. The singing in opera was phenomenal, the dancing in ballet unrivaled. But the singing and dancing in musical theater were usually mediocre. Chap had genius potential; he was another William Henry Fry in the making, as long as he eschewed burlesque. I worried that his accommodating impulses might derail him, his willingness to please roughnecks warping his talent. I guess I faced a similar challenge: In order to reach my highest potential, I had to toil in the lowliest circumstances, in trenches of blood and gold and politics.

As I walked up, two miners were fussing with Rosie outside her place. It was common for her to give readings to prospectors seeking a rich, hidden vein in the Comstock. It often happened that she directed them to worthwhile streams…but not always. In this case, the men wanted a refund for her predictive imprecision. Surly, crocked, and disheveled from a night of deranged behavior, they waved their arms emphatically, as if summoning before them the fruitless location that Rosie, through her stone, had suggested.

"Twern't nothing there!" the tall, lanky one said. "Only an endless skunk, three days long."

"You're a Mormon gypsy," the stout one scolded. "You got no business sending us into the dead spots. We need a pay streak, see?"

"Give us our money back or Jesse here is gonna slap the devil right outta ya!"

"Hell, I'll do *more* than slap her, Leonard," Jesse said, walking right up to Rosie threateningly.

Using a broom to fend them off, Rosie retreated only slightly, looking up at him with anger. "You're the kind that hits a woman. I see that now. You should be ashamed!"

"I don't hit *women*. But I'll happily strike a Mormon hussy with a fake seer rock who steals from the working man. Why, I should just—" He raised his arm to cuff her.

Before he could swing, I grabbed his wrist, twisting his arm behind his back and using my other arm to apply painful pressure to his neck. "You should just get sober, return to that part of the river she told you about, and look harder."

Unable to break free and identify who was wrenching his arm, Jesse called out to his buddy. "Leonard, get this maggot off me!"

"I—I can't rightly do that, Jesse," Leonard stammered.

"Ouch! Why the hell not?!" Jesse bleated, falling to his knees.

"It's the Kid."

"Kid? He's a biggun for a child and lookin' to break my arm."

"No, I mean he—he might do that and worse. That there's Kid Crimson."

This information seemed to clear Jesse's head. "We're in agreement with you, Kid. It's obviously a better notion to go back to that part of the river and scour it really good."

"We hit a streak of bum luck is all," Leonard insisted.

"Yessir, a skunk can turn into a golden goose overnight. Set me free, Kid, and we won't bother this young prophetess anymore."

I guided him back to his feet, then shoved him hard so that he collided with his friend, both of them toppling over onto the boardwalk. "Go on and *get*," I said. "Don't bother Rosie again until you find enough silver to drink yourself silly."

"Thanks, Kid," Leonard said, brushing the dust from his clothes and already heading in the direction of the Blood Nugget. "We'll follow your advice."

"We sure will—hey, okay, we're moving!" Jesse said, jumping out of the path of Rosie's swinging broom.

The two men quickly walked away, Rosie observing

them until they turned the corner. Then she turned to smile at me. "Glad you showed up, Kid. Sorry you had to be a bodyguard."

"Don't be. Those two jokers did me a favor, getting my blood flowing again after being in a coma for three days."

"Well then, happy to help out." She smiled, giving the sun a run for its money.

"Where's Chap?" I said. "He leave for the opera house early?"

"No, he's helping Winifred." She gave me a sly look, which I ignored. I couldn't fathom why bringing a working girl to Virginia City was affecting people's impression of me. They should have known I liked picking up strays. Which made me wonder how Dolly was faring with the Mormons, but I saved that thought for later. "Helping her with what?"

"They're moving a stove into her new place. She's opening a Cornish pasty joint."

"Wait, Winnie's a restaurateur now? I took a few days to recover and the whole world changed."

"Virginia City is a town of second chances," Rosie said, leaning her broom against the fence outside her apartment. "You know that as well as anyone, Kid."

"Okay, but Winnie has no money. Where'd she secure funds?"

"Ralston gave her a loan. He's what they call a food connoisseur."

I removed my hat to scratch my head. "Well, that's certainly true. Who made the connection?"

"Apparently, Ralston had done business in Silver Reef and recognized Winifred when she arrived. John Mackay, the Ophir superintendent, mentioned Winifred's pasty joint to the miners and they've already put in orders for next week."

"Amazing," I said. "Ralston the social reformer."

"I know why you're here, by the way."

I nodded. "Grover intimated that you saw something recently."

"Yes," she said, unpinning her hair so that it cascaded down her back like a blonde waterfall that stopped in the middle of her tailbone. She always did this before a peepstone session. "We should look again to make sure my interpretation is consistent."

"Last session didn't go so well," I reminded her. "You claimed to speak with my father."

She looked at me as if I had spat in her mashed potatoes. "Kid, did everything I related to you on that day eventually come to pass?"

"Yes," I said. "Everything."

"In that case, I'd say it went rather well."

"I don't understand why my father appears when I join you for a stone-gazing."

"He's watching over you; he wants to reunite."

"Impossible, I'm afraid. The living exist on one side, the dead on the other."

"It's not his spirit I'm communicating with, Kid," she said, biting her gorgeous lip as she placed her elegant fingers on my bruised jaw, her eyes blue as the ocean. "It's your father himself."

———

ROSIE HAD PREPARED for a peepstone session, the rock sitting in a cast-iron dutch oven pot on her kitchen table. We sat down across from one other and held hands. Even though all the trees had been stripped for firewood, I heard the rasping and descending notes of a butcherbird somewhere in the distance, piercing the clang and hum of mining equipment.

She closed her eyes and lowered her head to the stone to plumb the mystery of my near future.

"He's here," she said, raising her head from the pot. Like the last time, her eyes went white, her face taking on years even though I perceived no wrinkles or sagging flesh. Her flesh went icy cold and I had to stop myself from instinctively pulling away.

"What does he want? I can give him another bullet."

She didn't respond, instead lowering her head deeper and softly growling, snarling.

"Uh-oh. Rosie?"

She suddenly craned her neck and twisted her spine, as if suffering a seizure. "Guns are coming to Virginia City. *Big* guns."

"I already know that. What's his game, Rosie?"

"Bright white. They have deadly chemicals."

I assumed my father, if I *believed* this tomfoolery, was warning me, through Rosie, that Polignac planned to attack Virginia City at night using "limelights"—chemical lamps fueled by superheated balls of lime or calcium oxide to create an incandescent glow. By shining lights on our town, the French Rebs might easily target us while at the same time blinding everyone. "Okay, I think I understand. But can you ask him, Rosie? Ask him why he cares."

She stopped twisting in her chair, closed her eyes, and sat normally before taking a deep breath. Her hands felt like frozen steel fur traps in winter. "He insists you and he will be together again. He wants you to know that he's sorry. For all the pain. Tears. Everything."

Rage surged in my heart. My father was a liar, a

conniver, a demon pretending to be human. If he *were* still alive and roaming the earth, this is exactly what he would strive to do: worm his way into my life and destroy the people around me. "Rosie, I appreciate what you're trying to do. You're well-intentioned, but this is all nonsense."

Suddenly, she opened her eyes, black as midnight, and said, in a gruff voice similar to my father's, "Son, there are forces more sinister than the Confederacy pursuing you. They want to snuff the people around you and break your soul. Shield your loved ones, Kid. War is coming to Virginia City." Then she let her chin drop, let go of my hands, and began sliding out of her chair.

I caught her before she slumped to the floor. "Rosie, you need rest."

I picked her up in my arms and lay her slender figure on the tufted sofa in her living room. She was no longer frigid to the touch and her face returned to its usual state of loveliness. With my fingertips, I brushed her blonde hair from her forehead and covered her with a quilted blanket. I had to hand it to her, she made me wonder: Was Rosie a natural performer, playing the clairvoyant role to the hilt? Or was she truly a medium in contact with the spectral realm, possessing the ability to converse with cutthroats thousands of miles away?

"Kid," she said, opening her eyes, moist from exhaustion and fear. She didn't move from the sofa. "I'm so sorry."

"About what?"

"Your father. I—I can sense malignant desires in him."

"Rosie, honey, you have nothing to apologize for. In fact...well, we can talk about this later." Because for now, I needed to figure out how to prepare for the possibility of multiple cannons bombarding Virginia City before Polignac, fully armed, mobilized to attack us in order to thwart a Union victory. I had a few aces though. One of them was the escaped animal I'd seized from Dr. Skorpion and brought here.

HEAD BANDAGED, Ringmaster Clyde smoked a cigarette in his white undershirt and red pants and black boots, sitting on stacked, burlap bags of rice outside John John's house, which squatted on the edge of his pig farm, a muck-laden expanse nestled at the base of Sun Mountain. Clyde watched attentively as Sarah, wearing her rabbit skin dress and grass headpiece, approached the big cat from a secondary cage of iron up against the lion cage. Bars separated her space from the animal's but she was skinny enough to slip through them.

I gasped and nearly grabbed my pistol as she slowly insinuated her adorable head, then her tiny shoulders, through the bars. The only reason I hesitated was because the lion looked sleepy. He was lying down on his right side, covering one foot with the other, tail tucked between his thighs. This wasn't an angry or even hungry jungle cat. Still, it was madness to set foot inside a cage with a lion in it.

"Sarah, you dumb little donkey," I muttered, hoping I wasn't about to witness a horror scene.

Eventually, she worked her entire body into the cage to stare confidently at a bored, yawning lion. Clearly, she'd been working up to this moment in the last few days since my return, the lion now completely used to Sarah's presence within the same space.

"Good boy," she said, gradually turning sideways to

slide between the bars and return to the adjacent cage. The whole time she never took her eyes off the king of beasts.

When she was back in her own cage, she grabbed a pig tongue that had been sitting atop a stool and buzzing with flies and tossed it at the lion. He stood on all fours to gulp it down in one lazy bite before lying down again.

Ringmaster Clyde clapped. "Excellent, Sarah."

I was hot-headed about what I'd seen, which heightened my rudeness. "Clyde, Sarah isn't one of your circus freaks. She's a twelve-year-old girl. Wrangling dogs and pigs is one thing but training her to become a lion tamer is entirely different—and dangerous."

"That's funny," Clyde said, calmly blowing a smoke ring and clearly nurturing a grudge. "You stole one of my employees—a circus freak, as you call us—and put her into the line of fire."

"Nellie Brown," I said, trudging through the gunk to reach him, "is a fully grown woman."

Clyde shrugged. "You have a lot of people you feel responsible for. I respect that. But this isn't the vicious plantation you grew up on as a child, and you can't save everyone."

Who had this peanut slinger been talking to about my past? What was in that dime novel about me? I grabbed him by his shirt, knocked the cigarette from his mouth, lifted him off the rice sacks, and pushed him against the wall of John John's house. He didn't resist, knowing I'd smack him silly again. "You're a torrent of garbage."

I noticed something on the top of his hand. In the skin between his thumb and forefinger was a small tattoo that resembled the emblem of the Knights of the Golden Circle.

"Kid?" said a girl's voice behind me.

I turned to see Sarah and the lion outside their cages, the animal sitting on its rear haunches and staring at us, disinterested. I nearly fell over, pushing my shoulders against Clyde as he laughed at Sarah's alacrity. Fingers hovering above the butt of my Colt, I resisted taking aim, since she was in my line of fire.

"Sarah," I said, my voice quivering with anger and concern. "What are you doing, girl?"

"Preparing for the Rebs and their cannons," she said. "Soon I'll have my new friend ready to eat Frenchmen."

21

Word of an impending attack spread through Virginia City. Anxiety escalated, with people hoarding food, ammo, and medicated butt wipes that Mackay had shipped from Boston to cope with miners' recurring ringworm infections. Indeed, House of Hammers was cleaned out of essentials, only tools and mining equipment left on the shelves.

Miners continued their dirty work, occasionally pausing to ensure that an explosion detonated by a different gunpowder wasn't a Confederate cannon blasting at them or the town above. A number of residents didn't believe an attack was imminent, given last year's appearance of an Abraham Lincoln look-alike that fooled all of us into thinking the Great Emancipator had traveled to Virginia City to inspire the silver ore industry into generating more wealth for the Union. Even Bad Jace, who'd helped me blast butternut sympathizer Grinaker out of the sky with an improvised cannon housed in a mountain mineshaft, didn't think Polignac was worth worrying over.

"He's a watered-down shadow of Napoleon," Bad Jace said, back from his new job as the rail-station security director, drinking beers at the Blood Nugget with me and my newspaper pal Samuel Clemens. "The French haven't been the same since Bonaparte died in exile."

"The barbarian reads," Clemens muttered in my ear, "to my bewilderment."

The outlaw noticed, scowling. "What did you say, ink-slinger?"

"I said that my heart *bleeds* for the French people without a leader like Bonaparte." Clemens then proposed a toast.

In the spirit of the moment, the three of us raised our glasses to honor an empire builder, social reformer, and military legend.

"I'm relieved you're not intimidated by Polignac," I said to Bad Jace. "But I assure you that French Rebs are coming and bringing heavy guns."

Clemens cut in smoothly. "If nothing else, it makes delightful copy, which is the only thing I care about. After all, fighting against dangerous odds in Virginia City seems to be a common occurrence and I'm happy to fulfill my role as chronicler of the underdog Comstock. Whether this part of the world gets blown up or not, I'll be here to write down what happens."

"Or what *doesn't* happen," Bad Jace sneered. "You have a tendency, Missouri Man, to embellish the facts to an unwholesome degree."

"I've been called many things. But 'unwholesome' is by far my favorite adjective."

Bad Jace laughed and sipped his beer. "I'm starting to like you more."

They clinked glasses tipsily, then Clemens said, "In any case, look for my front-page article in tomorrow's

Territorial Enterprise. The headline reads: MORMON VS. OUTLAW IN OUTDOOR ARM-WRESTLING MATCH."

"Arm wrestling?" I wasn't sure I heard correctly, given the imminent gunpowder pounding from Polignac.

"No one told you? This afternoon, our gargantuan associate here is slated to twist wrists with another oversized fellow by the name of Rocker Portwell."

"What on earth! I was only sleeping off a smash to the face for two, maybe three, days. It seems everyone's mind snapped as I lay recovering."

"Your Mormon buddy," Bad Jace said, "is boastful and should be taken down a peg."

"I never heard exactly what prompted this conflict," Clemens said, lighting another cigar. "So I manufactured a conflict out of whole cloth."

"That's your third cheroot, Sam, and you're still nursing your first beer."

"Kid, if smoking isn't allowed in heaven, I'll stand outside the gates blowing tobacco halos."

"To get back to what started this arm-wrestling business," Bad Jace said. "We ran into each other at Roscoe's House of Hammers yesterday. He was asking Roscoe about a hacksaw he planned to use on the barrel of his Navy Colt. I told him that was a dumb idea and that he might as well grind the sights and wear a blindfold when he fires the pistol."

"Okay, but how does this translate into arm wrestling?"

"Well, then he claimed that sawing off the barrel makes it easier to hide a gun and that accuracy is rarely a problem when killing, for example, anti-Mormon governors. I mean, he acted as if he's the only one in Virginia City who's ever killed an elected official. I've killed plenty!"

A wide-eyed miner carrying two beers back to his table obviously heard the bizarre boast, ducking his head and walking by without daring to glance at any of us.

"Bad Jace," I said, rubbing my eyes. "Please lower your voice when speaking of such horrors. Especially in front of a muckraker like our friend Clemens here."

Clemens had whipped out his notepad, scribbling something down.

Bad Jace snatched it from his hands, silently scanning the page. "One dressed-out raccoon, one sliced onion," he recited, before throwing the pad at Clemens. "A recipe for raccoon fricassee."

"I wasn't paying attention because I'm hungry." Clemens smiled, signaling Jericho the bartender for another round.

"So because Rocker bragged about assassinating a politician, you're going to arm wrestle him?"

Bad Jace nodded. "Mormons have a chip on their shoulder. Also, I need to know if I can trust Rocker. Sure, you spent days on the trail together, but I need to assess him for myself."

"I can tell you that he picked up a Paiute warrior and tossed him like a sack of feed."

Bad Jace started to grab Clemens by his collar and belt as if to throw him. Feigning alarm, Clemens exclaimed, "Unhand me, you brute, and I won't publish your murder confession!"

"Share some of the fricassee with me and it's a deal."

They clinked empty glasses again.

Almost as if on cue, Jericho arrived, carrying fresh mugs of beers and smiling at our good time. "Kid, how are Sarah and the lion?"

I groaned. "I don't like Ringmaster Clyde. Something's not right about him, so I put a stop to her training. But to answer your question, Sarah is fearless and outrageous and much wilder than the lion. Or she's like Daniel in the Bible, with an angel keeping her safe. When Poppy finds out, she'll skin me."

Jericho laughed, left us to yak some more, then returned to serve us each a steaming-hot Cornish pasty on a wooden plate. "These are on the house. We're trying out a new vendor."

"You're kidding me," I said. "Are they—"

"They are," Jericho interrupted. "Winifred, the girl you brought from Silver Reef, bakes a mean meat pie."

Bad Jace ate half of his in a single bite, gasping from the heat.

Clemens used a fork to carve out a piece of the crimped edge, sampling it. "Scrumptious."

I pushed my plate away. "Is everyone now participating in a legitimate business in Virginia City... except me?"

"Not too late," Bad Jace said through a mouthful of pasty. "You can always marry Poppy or Verbena and co-own their establishments for them."

"A real suffragist *you* are," Clemens said, daintily forking a bite and chasing it with a sip of beer and a puff on his cigar.

"Oh, I'm *all* about making women suffer," Bad Jace guffawed.

At that moment, Lydia Sweet, the beautiful Oregon schoolteacher we'd rescued from the clutches of bandits outside Virginia City, came up behind him, placing her slender arms around his hairy neck. "Darling," she said. "Thank you for decorating my classroom earlier today. It looks superb! The children will absolutely love what you've done with the space."

If I'd had pasty in my mouth, I might've choked to

death. Clemens had to bury his laughter by turning his head and pretending to endure a sneezing fit.

"I, uh, I only helped out a little bit," Bad Jace said, trying to downplay his flair for beautification. "I don't think I've ever set foot inside a proper schoolhouse before."

"Well, let me just say that the origami roses you folded with red paper look fantastic."

Clemens whispered in my ear. "Origami? With those ham hocks for fingers?"

"Um, would you like some pasty, Lydia?" Bad Jace asked, trying to change the subject, but sheepish enough that she figured out that she was embarrassing him in front of his buddies.

"Oh, um, no thank you. I'll let you gentlemen enjoy your drinks and pasties. Dinner later, Jason?"

"Yes, ma'am." He didn't look at anyone now, focusing on his beer and snack as Lydia headed over to where Verbena was counting the till.

"Do you know," Clemens said, "what's worse than helping a woman decorate her classroom?"

Neither of us said anything, but the wordsmith was on a roll.

"When she transforms a perfectly good Bad into a perfectly bad Good. Or...when she turns a Fierce Jace into a Domesticated Jason."

Just before arm wrestling the strongest man in the West, I thought, and battling French cannons, Rebel mercenaries, and Union deserters. But I knew better than to say anything.

THE NEXT DAY, the arm-wrestling match drew more than five hundred people to the Blood Nugget. Verbena had asked Jericho to assemble a small wooden riser, two stools, and a high-top pub table for Bad Jace and Rocker to snap each other's wrists off in plain view of the crowd. Chaparral and Jericho pushed the piano out the saloon doors and onto the boardwalk, initiating even more gossip that the two arm wrestlers were so powerful that the Blood Nugget dare not live up to its name and risk splattering blood on everyone and everything inside the establishment.

"It is, of course, much easier to hose ichor off the C Street boardwalk than it is to scrub clean the wooden slats of a barroom floor," Clemens said to the forewoman of the Virginia City Miner's Wives' Cooking, Sewing, and Civilizing Club, while fanning himself with a folded-over copy of the *Territorial Enterprise* that featured his article. As he well knew would happen, Clemens's words spread like wildfire, even faster than the news of Polignac's imminent arrival, from the bottom of Sun Mountain to the peak of Mount Ophir, the womenfolk arriving en masse with protest signs that read: BLOOD IS *NOT* AMUSEMENT! and VOTES FOR WOMEN NOW!

One of the ladies carrying a protest placard was, oddly enough, schoolteacher Lydia Sweet, who smooched Bad Jace on his ruddy cheek and briefly massaged his shoulders before scurrying away to join the loudly jeering miners' wives, a platoon of clucking hens who believed the shady mining company, assisted by the corrupt town of Virginia City, conspired to underpay their husbands and suppress female agency at the polls.

As I looked over the ladies, I saw enterprising Ezra and adorable Sarah scooting under, around, and through the throng. Ezra carried a cowboy hat upside down to receive coins, while Sarah yelled in a high-pitched voice, "Twenty-five cents admission! Cough it up, you roughnecks!"

Chaparral took the bullhorn to announce, "There is to be *no* betting—I repeat, *no* betting on this match between the giants of Virginia City. All proceeds from this spectacle will go toward the building of a new schoolhouse on D Street! The wrestlers themselves are taking away nothing except bragging rights and sore appendages!"

"Appendages?" Verbena said, making a visor with her hand to shield her eyes from the sun. "He meant to say 'limbs,' didn't he?"

"An appendage *is* a limb," Clemens confirmed.

"I always thought it meant—oh, well, never mind." Her face turned beet red.

"Oh, Chap is being cheeky, all right," Rosie said, side-eyeing my beer.

"Rosie, here," I said, presenting it to her. "I haven't taken a single sip."

"Oh, I couldn't drink your cold pint, Kid."

I sighed and used my other hand to grab hers and place my beer in it. "Drink, woman. You'll never get the vote with that attitude."

Her eyes grew big and she took a big sip, then wiped her mouth with the sleeve of her dress. "I'll take a beer over the vote any day. What woman in her right mind wants to step into the polls now with so much horror happening in the eastern United States?"

"I don't know the first thing about voting and I don't value it."

"He seemed confident, Kid."

"Who did?"

"Your father."

I grunted. "Confident about what?"

"That you were going to have contact with him soon."

"We'll see," I said. "He wasn't, let's just say, in the greatest health last time we spoke."

Verbena had been standing in front of us and now turned to let us know with a huge smile, "They're starting!"

Bad Jace and Rocker Portwell scaled the stairs of the riser and took their positions, standing opposite each other at the table like silent stone-faced gladiators. Bad Jace wore black denim and a black cowboy hat, while Rocker looked farm-ready in blue denim overalls and a high-crowned straw hat. The crowd cheered as they got into position and Chaparral once again raised the horn.

"And now, to referee the match, I give you the prettiest flower in all of Storey County...the petal from Peking, the sunflower from the Sure Cure...the lovely... Poppy!"

A hush fell over the audience as my stunning Chinese girlfriend stepped forward in a pink flowing medieval-style tea gown made of taffeta and embroidered with chrysanthemum flowers. She looked like an aqueous dessert, a succulent morsel, if there ever was one.

The sun hung high in the sky, casting no shadows along the street as townsfolk continued to gather in front of the Blood Nugget's weathered wooden façade. The air was charged with anticipation, a vibration rippling through the crowd as the two titans of our little mining town stood face to face and rolled up their sleeves. Their biceps bulged. Their eyes were locked in a fierce gaze, confirming the intense rivalry between them.

The crowd pressed in, forming a half-circle around the makeshift arena, voices rising in a cacophony of cheers and jeers. Men in wide-brimmed hats and women in billowing skirts jostled for the best vantage to take in the impending showdown. Dust was kicked up from the street beneath their boots, adding to the scene's gritty atmosphere.

Up on the riser, Bad Jace was a towering behemoth, arms like tree trunks, beard bristling with menace. Rocker was a tad leaner, but no less formidable, with broad shoulders that made him look like a muscular grizzly, blue eyes gleaming with a ferocity that sent a shiver down the spine of many an onlooker. I sensed that Emma's capture had something to do with his desire for physical exertion and conquest. He was frustrated and saddened, and all he could do at the moment was try to rip another man's arm off.

With a grunt of exertion, the two men bellied up to the table and locked hands, fingers intertwining in a vise-like grip that promised immense pain and short-lived glory. The crowd fell silent again, holding its collective breath in the moments before the confrontation to come.

Poppy wrapped their hands together with a length of silk ribbon, then steadied and balanced their grip so that neither started with an advantage. When she was satisfied, she let the silence elongate before gritting her teeth and yelling, "Go!"

With a sudden explosive burst of energy, the match was underway.

Sinews strained, veins popped, and muscles bulged as Bad Jace and Rocker threw their weight into the contest, faces contorted in grimaces of determination. The screams from the crowd were hair-raising and infectious. Sweat poured from their brows as they fought for masculine supremacy. Inch by inch, they battled, neither willing to submit. The crowd erupted into a frenzy, rising to a roar as the struggle reached its climax. Tendons bulging beneath taut skin, the two men poured every ounce of their strength into the contest.

Finally, with a sudden lurch and an aggressive roar, Bad Jace slammed Rocker's hand down onto the table. The crowd exploded into cheers and several big miners hoisted Bad Jace onto their shoulders in a jubilant celebration of his victory. Beer went flying into the air, splashing everyone and causing the suffragettes to run for cover.

Even in defeat, Rocker remained unbowed, eyes burning with a fierce pride that spoke of violence yet to come. With a nod of respect to his opponent, he disappeared with Elders Wilford and Spencer—the three of them no doubt chomping at the bit to kill Polignac—into the swirl of ecstatic onlookers, leaving behind the memory of a battle well fought.

"What do you think of the power of the pen, Kid?" Clemens said to me as I checked my coat for wet spots from all the sloshed beer. "My article generated quite a turnout."

"Today's *Territorial Enterprise*," I said, "was displayed and distributed, what, four hours ago?"

Clemens nodded. "That's all the time we need to get the town mobilized. I'll have the papers printed this afternoon and ready to dispense at a moment's notice. The headline will read: VIRGINIA CITY BRACES FOR REB ATTACK. If you send someone to scout Polignac, we can have everyone armed, sheltered, and ready to repulse the Confederate assault."

If you want something done right, I thought, do it yourself. To Clemens, I said, "I'll scout the bastard."

22

I HAD JUST FINISHED SADDLING MY APPALOOSA when Ezra came running into the livery to tell me Poppy and Verbena were squabbling again. Between the shoeshine boy's breathless eruption and my putting two and two together as I ran to the Blood Nugget, I inferred that the disagreement had something to do with the revenue generated from all the beer sold at the arm-wrestling event. Poppy encouraged Verbena to give a percentage of the money to the new school that Lydia Sweet was hoping to build. Verbena found this a bold suggestion coming from someone who pushed opium on impoverished war veterans, and what schoolteacher would want donations from a drug peddler?

Throwing fists and yanking one another's hair, they'd cleared the Blood Nugget of patrons who didn't want to be anywhere near a catfight involving Kid Crimson's friends, which is probably why a banker had neglected to tip Ezra, hurrying away due to the commotion and knives flashing. I entered the saloon to find Winnie with a couch pillow fending off Poppy's slashing blade and

Lydia Sweet using a serving tray to keep Verbena's steak knife at bay.

I fired my pistol. The noise was deafening and startled the women enough so that they paused their fighting. "Ladies," I said, "your behavior is unacceptable. The *real* enemy—French Rebs with deadly cannons—are likely to attack Virginia City at any moment. We can't have our best residents brawling over something as tedious as money."

"*My* behavior?" Poppy said, jaw clenched. "Kid, you bring a Silver Reef whore to town—a woman who I *know* for a fact gave you an intimate bubble bath—and you get her a job making meat pies for a saloon owner who's in love with you, and you tell me that *I'm* unacceptable?" She threw her knife in my direction, hitting a support column, handle thrumming from the impact.

"Tell your girlfriend," Verbena sneered, taking a turn, "that she has no business advising *me* how to contribute *my* hard-earned beer revenue to a schoolhouse-in-progress, when she doesn't even run a social business. Her customers hide in the dark on mattresses on the floor and get high as the moon without talking to anyone around them. She thinks she's *helping* those lost souls!" Then she threw her own blade, a heavy carving knife, that came close to hitting me but instead clanged against a table behind me.

"Kid," Winnie whined, "I appreciate you bringing me to Virginia City, but honestly you should take me back to Silver Reef now if this is what I can expect from people here."

"Thank God," Lydia Sweet huffed, puffing air into her bangs, "these women haven't reproduced and I don't have to worry about teaching their temperamental children for several years."

Verbena was incensed. "You miserable bi—"

"Look," I said. "I realize we're all tense due to a looming threat of invasion, but if we— "

Suddenly, the chandelier above me—a wire holding one of its brass fixtures severed by my bullet—came crashing down on my head. I retained consciousness, but the impact brought me to my knees and had me seeing stars.

"I need to start wearing a dragoon helmet," I said, touching my hair and checking my hand for blood. "Anyone seen my hat?"

"Oh, poor Kid!" Winnie said, in a voice that sounded reserved for lost kittens. She and Lydia Sweet came to my aid, each one taking an arm and guiding me into a chair. Verbena immediately tugged my boots off while Poppy inspected my scalp for cuts before announcing, "He'll have a knot, for sure."

"He just needs a bath," Winnie said. "I always feel better after a scrub."

"I have water boiling already," Poppy said. "Let's bring him across the street to the Sure Cure."

"I've been dying," Lydia Sweet said, "to try this new Marseille soap I picked up in Denver. I swear it smells like strawberries and cucumbers."

"I once won first place in a drink-mixing contest," Verbena said, "by using exactly those ingredients—plus gin, elderflower liqueur, and aromatic bitters. It tastes so summery!"

"I'm warm enough now to try a glass of that!" Winnie insisted.

"I'll make a pitcher right now for us to share. Kid, you'll love the taste of it!"

"Unnecessary, ladies, I'm fine. It's just a bump on my noggin. Alcohol will only…"

It was no use. Soon, I was sitting naked in a tub of warm water as Poppy and Winnie, wearing only their lace camisoles and flimsy knickers and nothing else, soaped my chest and nether regions as they sipped pink sugary drinks and listened to Lydia Sweet and Verbena, topless and stripped to their ruffled drawers, read aloud from various clothing catalogs shipped from Boston, laughing at the descriptions. My head hurt so badly from the chandelier that I couldn't enjoy it.

"Sorry I overreacted, honey," Verbena said to Poppy.

"I should apologize too," Poppy said.

They kissed and Verbena closed her eyes before placing her head between Poppy's perfect breasts as my girlfriend used her fingers to gently stroke the saloon owner's long chestnut hair.

Meanwhile, Lydia Sweet and Winnie drew snugly together to tangle their slender arms and drink from the other's strawberry-cucumber gin fizz.

"Lord," I lamented, "why does this only occur when I'm injured?"

"He needs more scrubbing, Poppy doll," Winnie said, removing Lydia Sweet's silk undershirt and then licking her shaved armpit.

Without getting up from her chair or putting down her drink—and with Verbena snoring on her collarbone—Poppy winked lasciviously at me. She elevated her sculpted leg to press her sexy foot against my chest, massaging me with her gorgeous toes.

"How much did you end up raising for the new school after the arm-wrestling exhibition?" I asked Lydia Sweet, as Winnie filled the schoolteacher's bellybutton with gin and sipped it.

"Enough for Ralston to agree to loan us the rest," Lydia Sweet said, gasping from the tongue-bathing pleasure that Winnie was inflicting on her navel…and other areas of her body.

"It's deeply inspiring," I said, "to witness Virginia City developing into a refined municipality."

BETWEEN THE THREE baths I'd enjoyed in the last ten days, I was the cleanest I'd been in years. I was also motivated to locate the French Confederate general, even if my head ached from the chandelier drop and, sadly, not from drinking too many strawberry-cucumber gin fizzes with the nubile women of Virginia City.

I considered bringing Rocker and the Mormons with me, but I knew I moved better, more quietly, by myself. Also, Polignac had made it personal for me.

I had my favorite horse under me and the morning temperature was ideal for riding. The spicy odor of pinyon trees reminded me that life was good, that evil might defeat humanity yet never be strong enough to vanquish nature. The world wouldn't end no matter how much gunpowder miners packed into the mountains, no matter how many cannons we built and fired at people and into mining towns. The earth was eternal and, centuries from now, another young man would stand here and think the same thoughts, feel the same sensation. Knowing this gave me confidence, made me feel I was destined to locate Polignac and bring him to ruin. He was crafty and violent, but so was I.

My horse stepped his way cautiously over rocky terrain. I only heard the rhythmic crunch of hooves striking the parched earth. Despite the solitude, I stayed vigilant, my senses honed by years spent hunting and tracking animals in the swamps of Georgia. Every shadow, every distant sound presented the possibility of danger, and I had to be ready to conceal, evade, or kill. The day wore on, my search leading me into a series of basins, luring me deeper into the heart of Nevada, specifically Sixmile Canyon Road, winding through the Flowery Range, a wildflower-festooned paradise shaded by cottonwood trees and paralleled by the seasonal Sixmile Creek, sheer cliffs rising toward the infinitely blue sky with biblical resplendence.

I knew that finding Polignac and his cannons was a challenge. After all, the rugged terrain provided too many concealment opportunities. But I was determined, driven by a vendetta against him for trying to kill me with a Derringer in Winnie's bedroom, but also by my duty to defend the people I loved—Poppy, Grover, Ezra, Sarah. The longer I went without pinpointing Polignac, the sooner his cannons arrived to smash the living daylights out of Virginia City. Indeed, with every passing hour, my commitment grew, fueled by the responsibility resting on my shoulders. The fate of my surrogate family depended on success. Failure wasn't an option.

Finally, a sign. When the sun reached its highest point, I halted my horse atop a ridge to scan the desert expanse below. In the distance, I spotted a faint dust cloud rising into the sky, a telltale sign of movement. With renewed purpose, I urged the Appaloosa forward, following the trail deeper into the canyons.

Shadows began to lengthen as the day waned. And then it happened: I caught sight of an encampment nestled in the wash.

Dismounting quietly, I approached with caution, my hand resting on the butt of my Colt. Drawing closer, I recognized the gray uniforms of Confederates, campfires flickering in the twilight. Among them, seated beside a fire, was the man I was seeking.

I counted fifty men, not an insignificant number, but hardly the overwhelming force I expected him to throw against the mining town of Virginia City, which boasted a total population of 4,000.

Also, I spotted only a single cannon, the one the frog and his platoon of Rebs and Union deserters and now French mercenaries—I spotted at least a dozen of them in his revitalized platoon—had stolen from the Mormon steelworks in Goblin Valley.

This wasn't what I expected and, as I started to slip away into the shadows, I noticed that a few of the wagon bonnets bore the branding of a circus company—but not Ringmaster Clyde's Circus Southwest outfit. It was another name, Celestial Circus.

What the heck was Polignac up to now?

I was moving to the clutch of pinyon trees where I'd tethered my horse when I saw someone heading to the same spot. It was one of Polignac's men on a security patrol, and I had a piece of luck. Behind the soldier, a coyote sprinted after a jackrabbit, scattering a group of mountain quail, their wings flapping noisily behind him. This gave me a chance to edge along the wall of the outer canyon and club him with the barrel of my Colt. I wasn't quick enough and bashed his teeth in, but his scream came out a toothless groan, and before he could squeeze off a warning shot, I punched him unconscious, putting him into the dust. I unsheathed my knife and placed the tip of the blade above his heart.

I thought about killing him, but as the last light of the day faded, I peered into his face and saw that he was a young man, younger than myself, and I didn't see the point. I'd seen nothing—no cannons, no chemical lights, no massive force of French mercs, only one cannon—and Polignac would know this when the soldier reported our skirmish to his general. This wasn't much of an assault that Polignac was leading, fizzling out here in Sixmile Canyon, much like the Confederate army itself.

I was putting away the knife when a figure jumped from the limbs of the pinyon tree that my horse was tied to, putting me in a full nelson, immobilizing me for a moment.

Only for a moment, though. The person was forty pounds lighter than me and I bucked him off, elbow-cracking him in the temple and getting the upper hand by putting my full weight on him and squeezing his throat in an attempt to cut off his oxygen.

He was soft, however, in all the wrong places. And I soon realized that I wasn't pitted against a man, but against a strong 120-pound woman instead. As soon I knew this, I felt the slight pinch of a knife blade pressing the flesh of my lower back, where my kidney was located.

"Kid," Nellie hoarsely whispered, my cruel fingers on her windpipe. "You came back for me."

23

I GRABBED HER HAND AND LIFTED HER OFF THE ground. "I'm not here for you," I said gruffly. "I'm tracking your husband, who I intend to kill before he bludgeons Virginia City with cannon fire."

Saucer-eyed, she opened her mouth in disbelief. "How—how did you—"

"I told you." I raised my voice. "I work for the government, Nellie. Pinkertons and US Marshals know all about you and Polignac. How could you keep that information from me?"

"Kid, you have to believe me. I had no idea he'd been deployed out west. I assumed he was in Louisiana, fighting the Union in Baton Rouge."

"He's a sadistic unconscionable cutthroat, Nellie. How did you end up marrying such a philistine?"

"New Orleans got worse, not better, when the war kicked off. Slaves didn't just turn on their owners, Kid. They came after anyone they perceived to be too light-skinned or an Uncle Tom. French citizenship was tempting and Polignac dangled it before me."

I couldn't believe what I was hearing. It made me feel sick and betrayed and I wanted to introduce my fist to her front teeth. Of course, I could never hit a woman. Watching my father brutalize my mother with his dirty mitts made it impossible for me to inflict violence on the fairer sex. Especially a black woman who resembled my mother. Indeed, Polignac was eerily similar to my father, a white man who desired a dark-skinned woman to physically hurt, to mentally torture. Despite the abuse, my mother loved the old man—to my shame and horror. It was likely no different for Nellie. I worshipped her like I did my mother. I wanted to save her from her own errant heart and I couldn't.

The pain I experienced from all this was unbearable. My face contorted, my lungs heaved, and it was all I could do to refrain from howling at the moon like a rabid coyote.

"Kid?" Nellie reached out and ran her fingers along my cheek, slowly bringing me around.

I tried to clear my head by shaking it violently. "I'm sorry, Nellie. You don't owe me any explanations for what you did to survive. I'm just...angry that you didn't fill me in when I first mentioned his name."

She sat down, her back against the trunk of a cottonwood, pulled her knees to her chest, and stared at the sun's fading embers. "At first, I didn't know who you and Bad Jace were chasing. I assumed our mission was exactly what you said it was, scouting Goblin Valley for weapons. I never anticipated running into my husband and every time I thought to bring him up, something got in the way."

"You're still married?"

Nellie covered her face with her hands. "It was always just a formality. Although I was his wife, his property really, he was never my husband. Then, when he went off to fight...I think they call it 'abandonment.' I took the opportunity to flee to greener pastures."

"Which means you lost your shot at French citizenship."

"Yes."

"And now you're stuck here in the United States, a nation engulfed by war."

She shrugged. "War is everywhere, Kid. France fights Prussia, expanding its empire. Italy is in the midst of its third war of independence. Russia is fighting Poland. There's no hiding from the insanity of armed conflict. Best way to deal with it is to prepare."

"That's why you took up knife throwing? Readied yourself for a world at war?"

"Yes. You did the same with your gun."

I hesitated to reveal the truth. I still had to ask her about the Knights of the Golden Circle emblem on her blade. But I went ahead and said, "Picking up the gun is the only reason I'm talking to you."

She nodded. There was nothing more for us to say on the matter.

"When did you escape? How did you escape? Where are Dolly and Emma?"

"During the confusion of yesterday's massacre, when Polignac and his men leveled Silver Reef, one of our guards got too close. Dolly tripped him, he fell right into me, and I, uh, relieved him of the keys to the locks on our chains." She smiled grimly. "Dolly latched on to some Silver Reef survivors heading up north. She wanted to stay with us, but we convinced her she should find some peace with a Mormon family. Emma is in a slot canyon on the other side of this valley, waiting for me."

I was speechless, not knowing where to begin.

"Apparently, Polignac still has feelings for me and made it known that any man who touched a hair on our heads would pay. One tried, with Emma. The three of us screamed so loud...well, it didn't turn out so good for the soldier, a Union deserter. Polignac had plans for us after the Virginia City campaign, but I wasn't about to stick around to find out what they were. I came back to assassinate him and then you showed up."

My stomach flopped. "Did you say Silver Reef was leveled?"

According to Nellie, it was a test run, a warm up for what Polignac aimed to do in Virginia City. For the smaller town, he arranged the cannons at the base of the mountain, within the city limits and across from the mines. When sunrise peeked its first rays of light on the horizon and the miners began trudging up the mountain to drop into their shafts, the French Reb general unleashed hell, blasting mining equipment to shards and sealing the mines in rubble.

Then he turned the cannons—all ten of them—on the town, leveling the saloon and Assay Office, obliterating the entirety of the main street with relentless fire. There was no chance for townfolk to surrender. As they ran, his French mercenaries descended—scalping, tormenting, killing. It was over in thirty minutes, a pocket of civilization wiped clean off the map.

"Good God. Those poor people. What did they ever do to deserve what happened to them?" My blood was starting to boil, heating up the monster that would soon need unleashing on these inhuman murderers.

"Oh, and the cannons are on their way to Virginia City as we speak."

"How's that? There's nothing here, Nellie. I even checked the canyon's other side."

"The guns aren't with Polignac, Kid. They're traveling in a separate caravan."

"What caravan?"

"Celestial Circus."

That was how Polignac managed to wheel cannons up to the base of the mountain, making it easy for him to sight the buildings in town and the silver mines at the top of the sandstone formations. "The people of Silver Reef thought the circus had arrived."

"Instead of animals and acrobats," Nellie said, "they got total destruction."

"One silver mine out of play, hitting Lincoln in the pocketbook."

And now the circus was headed to Virginia City, where Ezra and Sarah were waiting to the greet traveling entertainers who were really French mercs with a cannon in every wagon.

"We must stop Polignac here, Nellie," I said. "We can't wait for him to reach my girl Poppy."

"No, Kid. We need to intercept the caravan of cannons before it arrives in Virginia City. We leave now—no dallying."

I considered this and decided she was right. Polignac might be here, but the weapons might be deployed without him, killing everyone I held dear. I wasn't about to let that happen.

"Fine," I said. "One more question."

"Yes?" She stood up to brush the dust from her jeans.

"Knights of the Golden Circle. You had the emblem on one of your knives."

"My wedding gift. It's a terrific blade, a perfect throwing weapon. Polignac is a member. They're heavily bankrolled by industrialist sympathizers up north, looking to cut Lincoln at the knees by shutting down his silver supply."

I measured this explanation. "Where's your horse?"

"A hundred yards in that direction," she said, pointing.

I grabbed the reins of my own animal and climbed into the saddle, motioning for Nellie to join me so I could bring her to her mount. "I hope you like riding at a straight-from-hell gallop."

"Know what else I like?" she said, using a boulder to step up and situate herself behind me on the leather padding.

"Go on."

"Killing my husband and claiming his fortune—and citizenship."

NELLIE TOOK the lead and seemed to know where she was going.

We pushed our horses hard and fast, rocketing across a landscape that stretched on endlessly, a vast expanse of raw wilderness that had beckoned prospectors to unearth its hidden treasures. I was admiring its haunting beauty when I heard the crack of rifles behind us.

We'd been spotted by the French Rebs.

I reined in, looked back, and spied two riders on horseback, their silhouettes stark against the final fiery hues of the setting sun, hooves of the animals thundering across the arid terrain, dust clouds billowing.

The riders spurred their steeds onward and I sensed their hatred, hotter than the sun, simmering against my back. Gunfire echoed off canyon walls and mingled with the noise of our horses, creating a symphony of chaos. Bullets whizzed through the air like hornets.

The landscape around us blurred as we raced across the desert floor, red rock formations and twisted juniper trees passing by in a blur. Finally, the sun dipped below the horizon, casting the world into twilight as the riders pressed their attack, rifles blazing.

"Slot canyon!" Nellie called out and turned abruptly into a wash.

Staying on my horse, I threaded the gap and followed her into a narrow channel, dust and debris filling the air as bullets tore into the sandstone around us, rock shards cascading down from the cliffs above.

"On second thought, we had better odds in a flat-out race," I said. "Now we're like fish in a barrel."

"Hardly. You have guns and can shoot back. And *I*," she said, pulling two blades from her knife bandolier, "prefer to get up close."

"Don't let *me* stop you."

We got off our horses and tethered them to cottonwood behind some boulders.

The mercs didn't waste any time, the crunch of their approaching boots jangling my nerves as we concealed our snorting and winded horses behind a cluster of lichen-covered boulders.

I used a cutout between two rocks to draw a bead on the first one to make it up the wash. I fired two shots, missing with both, but sending him ducking behind a stand of pinyon, hoping to obscure himself. The smell of gunpowder and the odor of sweat and fear created a heavy tension in the air.

He popped out to unload his Winchester at my protected nest and I smiled, knowing what was about to happen.

Nellie gave a war cry, leaping from the top of the sandstone cliff in the merc's blind spot. She slashed his spine, then, as he swung his rifle to bash her, she sliced his heel tendon, completely incapacitating him as he tumbled into the dust spurting blood.

At this point, the second merc ran into the wash, tackling Nellie with such force that I saw her lose consciousness from getting knocked against a rock. He raised his rifle, poised to smash her with the heavy wooden stock. But I'd already advanced from the boulders, using my Colt to shoot him in his shoulder, then pouncing.

He tossed sand into my eyes, blinding me, then said, "*L'heure de mourir.*" Time to die.

He punched me so hard that my knees buckled and I lost my gun. I managed to block his roundhouse strike with my forearm, but the momentum of his attack sent me backpedaling until I found myself caught in a cul-de-sac. He had the reach and weight advantage, slamming me into the sandstone, so he could wind up and use me for a punching bag.

The merc delivered an uppercut to my jaw, still sore from Polignac hitting me with a curtain rod a week ago. Head ringing and vision blurring, I stomped the Frenchman's toes with my boot and he hollered in agony.

We each had our hands around the other's throat and he had the better grip. Soon the lights would go out and I'd be at his mercy.

"*Mourir, garçon,*" he hissed.

Suddenly, there was a blast and a bullet ripped through his hip, shattering bone. He screamed, pressing his hands to his pelvis to stanch the blood, but there was no chance for him. The artery was devastated. He collapsed to the ground, exsanguinating and twitching.

As my eyes adjusted, I looked behind me and standing there, Derringer still pointing straight out, but shaking like an aspen leaf in the wind, was Emma. Her face contorted, she croaked, "Where's Nellie? Is she okay? Please tell me she's okay. Please!"

"I'm sure she is," I said, walking over and squatting on my heels to look her in the eyes. "She just got knocked around a bit. Where did you come from?"

"Nellie left me here this afternoon. She told me to wait and she'd be back soon."

Nellie staggered up behind her, placing a hand on Emma's shoulder and subtly yet assuredly removing the pistol from her quivering hands. "Thanks for your help, little mama."

"I didn't mean to kill him! That's why I shot him in the leg. I'm sorry!"

"You didn't kill him, honey."

"I didn't?"

"No. He killed himself," I said, "by doing someone else's dirty work. Do you have a horse?"

Emma nodded, indicating it was tethered and waiting at the deep end of the canyon.

"Wait here. I need to breathe." Nellie trudged up to the top of the cliff wall and looked back at where the two Frenchmen had come from.

When she half-ran back down, I asked, "Anyone else on the way?"

She shook her head. "Not yet. We should move, Kid."

"How fast are you on a mount?" I asked Emma.

"Not as fast as you. But I've been riding horses and shooting pistols since I was a child."

"So." I tried to smile, but my jaw was out of whack and my head felt like a bell being rung, over and over. "Sounds like you had a fun time being a Mormon." We saddled up our horses again and I boosted Emma into a spot on the saddle behind Nellie.

"Yes, but I want to try living in Virginia City. Can I?"

"Sure. You'll love it. Well, except for men exploding the mountain in search of silver."

"I want to make money too."

"What for?" Nellie asked her.

"For myself. I still follow the church, but there's more to life than marriage. Life is too short."

"Good girl," I said, slapping the reins and moving my Appaloosa through the rest of the canyon.

"I changed my mind, Kid. I'm *not* sorry I shot that man. He was going to hurt you and Nellie."

"He was."

"Next time I shoot a bad guy, I'll aim for the heart."

"Save some bad guys for me!" I joked.

"I think," Nellie mumbled, rubbing the back of her head where it hit the wall, "there are enough for the two of you."

24

We rode like the devil, galloping for an hour across rough terrain as sunrise pinked the sky. We didn't stop and we didn't talk, choking on trail dirt and pushing our poor horses to their limits.

Before leaving town to scout Polignac, I'd asked Poppy for a favor, a task that only she could complete. I was hoping that my suspicions were wrong, but I couldn't help noticing something odd about Ringmaster Clyde's behavior during his lion-training session with Sarah. Also, his tattoo resembled the insignia of the Knights of the Golden Circle. On top of this, I'd noticed another fresh grave in the Chinese cemetery that Grover couldn't account for. In other words, I had a hunch that Clyde's story about being ambushed might be more—or less—complicated than I'd initially considered.

These questions were pushed aside when we saw two riders approaching on the horizon, dust cloud billowing. We reined our horses and looked at one another, trying to decide our next move.

"Fight or run?" Nellie asked.

"The way they ride," I said. "Looks familiar."

"That's my brother, Spencer!" Emma exclaimed, balling her fists with delight.

Nellie squinted. "Is the other one Rocker?"

"No, it's my very worst friend in the world." I made a clicking sound, my horse taking off toward the duo.

Sure enough, as we got closer, the size and shapes of the riders resolved into Bad Jace and Elder Spencer. They didn't look happy and neither did their horses, good and lathered.

"Your expression is scaring me, gentlemen," I huffed, out of breath, my Appaloosa rearing from our sudden stop.

"Well, your disappearance scared us, Kid." Bad Jace's face was drenched in sweat, a bandolier swathed around his chest stuffed with cartridges.

I shook my head. "Why the hell are you way out here?"

"Looking for you!" Spencer removed his straw hat to wipe his brow.

"Why?"

"Strangeness everywhere," Bad Jace said.

"Like what?"

"For one, another clown gathering, only this one was unexpected. Celestial Circus. Ever hear of it?"

"Hear of it!" I reached out with one arm to grab him by his denim shirt. "Don't you dare let them in!"

He knocked my arm away and stared at me like I required a straitjacket. "What? Why the hell not?"

Then Elder Spencer noticed who was cantering up behind me. "Is that my dear sister?"

"Spencer!" Emma called out, reining her horse at the last moment, her mount bumping mine. She hopped off the saddle, her brother doing the same, and they embraced.

"Did they hurt you, sis?"

"No, Nellie kept me safe."

"Thank you," Spencer said to the knife thrower as she rode up to join us. His voice seemed on the verge of breaking. "I-I don't know how to repay you, Nellie."

"Help me kill my husband for starters," she said coldly.

Bad Jace spat out his plug. "This conversation," he said, "is taking a dark turn."

"Where's Rocker?" Emma asked.

"Ralston sent him and Elder Wilford to search the area for Polignac."

"The insane frog is right behind us," I said. "Let's get to town and dismantle that fake circus before they launch an attack."

"Fake? What do you mean?"

"They're not acrobats and performers. They're mercenaries on Polignac's payroll. And they've ditched the caged animals in favor of cannons."

"You mean the circus carriages are freighting—"

"Heavy guns," I finished Bad Jace's thought for him

Bad Jace and Spencer looked at each other in horror.

"Where's the circus setting up?"

"Ralston says he never booked it," Bad Jace said, "and the main road to town is blocked by an overturned ore cart that Mackay is trying to clean up. So Ralston had the circus set up over by the sawmill."

"Good," I said. "That's on the outer edge of Sun Mountain. Not a great vantage for firing guns at Virginia City."

"But the miners are demanding that the caravan be

allowed in the city next to the Chinese graveyard. They're hankering to see the tattooed lady."

"Tattoos?" Emma said. "On a woman?"

"Godless gentiles," Spencer muttered.

The sound of hooves thundered in the distance, getting louder by the moment.

"Here they come," Nellie said.

Bad Jace took field glasses from his saddle to scan the horizon. "Looks like twenty. No, thirty."

"Fifty, at least." An image of Polignac's cannonballs pounding Virginia City to smithereens and killing Ezra and Sarah and Poppy and Grover suddenly flashed before my eyes. If only there was some way to warn everyone, to alert Rocker and Chaparral and the others.

As if reading my frantic mind, Nellie made a kissing noise and leaned forward on her horse, taking off in the direction of Virginia City.

The rest of us followed, struggling to keep up. Nellie's steed, even after a long ride, was faster than double-struck lightning.

"That's a speedy animal!" I called out to Emma.

"It's Polignac's!" She had one hand on the reins, the other securing her windblown bonnet.

"Nellie stole his horse?"

Emma laughed. "She doesn't like him anymore! Not husband material!"

We rode, hard, for another hour until we could see Virginia City in the distance, the peaks of the Virginia Range casting ominous shadows over the squat wooden buildings. Even above the sound of our galloping horses, I could hear familiar noises—the clanging of pickaxes against rock, the shouting of men, and the creaking of ore-laden wagons. It was galling to see the town behaving as if everything were normal, when in fact every inhabitant was in danger of getting blown to Kingdom Come.

We picked up the main road, where the miners were still picking up the ore that had fallen from the overturned cart. We gave the accident a wide berth and trotted into the muddy streets of town, people ignoring us as life continued on its usual course. A few faces popped up to examine us momentarily before falling away as everyone hustled to make a buck in a place where everything of value was stripped away, leaving nothing but a barren wasteland, empty whiskey bottles, and simmering greed. Looking around, I wondered why I was so committed to defending a congregation of rapacious fools.

My disgust was dispelled by Ezra, the shoeshine boy, whom Poppy and I loved as if he were our own, running along the boardwalk toward us and waving to get my attention. "Kid! Poppy told me to bring you straight to her when you showed up!"

"Can't right now," I told him. "I have to confront some circus performers."

"That's what she wants to see you about, Kid. The circus!"

Bad Jace wasn't going to wait for me. "Word has it they've been let inside the town and have set up at Sun Mountain. Nellie and I will scout them."

"Emma and I," Spencer said, "will search for Rocker and Wilford."

I nodded, then said to Ezra, "Tell Sam Clemens to print his newspaper right away. French Rebs are already here."

Ezra raced toward the *Territorial Enterprise* office, nearly getting smashed by a cart and horses when he crossed C Street without looking.

I reached the Sure Cure, tethered my Appaloosa to the post, and went inside.

POPPY'S OPIUM establishment was dim and reeked of vinegar, of all strange smells. There wasn't a single customer in the place and when my eyes adjusted to the darkness, I saw that she was using a broomstick to stir a steel tub of water. Something was in the tub, clanging against the sides with every churning motion she made.

"Odd time to be cleaning the Sure Cure, my flower. Just before our town gets bombarded."

"I'm not cleaning," Poppy said. "I'm defusing." Several strands of long black hair in her face and the rest tied with red ribbon in a low bun, Poppy looked devourable in a sleeveless black-butterfly muslin dress, her sculpted arms causing my chest to tighten. She wore green silk embroidered sandals, closed toe, careful not to splash with whatever she was sloshing around.

"Poppy, you look exquisite no matter what you're doing."

"King Zhou, John John's gunpowder-detecting hog, found these," she said, leaning the broom against the wall to greet me with a hug. "I missed you, Kid." She stood on her toes to kiss me.

I held her tightly, never wanting to let go. But I had only a moment before preparing to confront the French Rebs on the edge of Sun Mountain. "What are we looking at? What did the pig find, darling?"

"Someone was burying cannonballs in the Chinese graveyard. After King Zhou sniffed them out, Uncle John John and I wheelbarrowed as many as we could over here to the Sure Cure. We're soaking them in vinegar and water to neutralize the black gunpowder."

"Who's burying cannonballs in a graveyard?"

"I don't know, but Sarah shared her suspicion this morning and I haven't seen her since."

My fists clenched in burgeoning fury. "You don't have to say it. Where's Ringmaster Clyde, Poppy?"

"You think he's the one—"

"Sarah figured him out, Poppy. He's either killed her or he's keeping her somewhere."

"Kid, I think you're right," she said, her hands trembling against my chest. "She told me his bandage isn't covering a wound. He was never injured." Poppy stifled a sob.

"Stop weeping, baby. Grab your rifle and meet me at Clyde's cabin," I said, picking up a dry cannonball with a wooden fuse that she hadn't yet soaked.

Eyes moist with anger, Poppy undid the ribbon in her hair, placing it in her mouth to put it up on top of her head. "If he's hurt Sarah, Kid, I'll...I'll..."

"We'll get her back, Poppy." I embraced her again and kissed her forehead.

Ezra burst into the Sure Cure, out of breath. Poppy had a rule that he could never set foot inside her establishment under any circumstances, so we knew it had to be urgent. "Kid, that weird circus ringmaster kidnapped my girlfriend!"

"Where is she? Do you know?"

"Chinese graveyard."

"Let's go. You're both coming with me. Poppy, we'll take your carriage."

"Kid, no! We can't take Ezra."

"He was with me in the hot-air balloon. This is nothing compared to that."

"I hope your words," Poppy said, ramming a ball into her percussion revolver, "aren't famous or last."

EZRA BROUGHT Poppy's buckboard wagon around back and we hopped in. He slapped the reins and we were off, the trenches and potholes of D Street jostling us off our seats and causing me to hold down my hat and grip the side rail to keep from falling into the mud.

Someone on crutches hobbled into the road, waving us down and shouting, "Kid!"

"Stop the cart, Ezra." Clearly, whoever this was wanted a word with me. As we got closer, he looked familiar, but I couldn't place him. Then it hit me. It was the Arkansas boy, Foster, one of Polignac's Rebel soldiers, whose life I spared outside of Father Ephraim's caves.

Poppy looked from Foster to me and back to Forster, then asked, "Kid, did you break that man's leg?"

"No. Well, maybe a little."

Ezra pulled on the reins, stopping the buggy, allowing the man to three-leg it over to me. I placed my hand on the grip of my Colt. I had no idea what he wanted and though he was hobbled, I wasn't taking any chances.

"Crimson," Foster said. "I wanted to thank you again. I—I'm no longer with Polignac."

"You're welcome and I'm glad to hear you've come to your senses. Thing is, we're in a hurry. So if you'll excuse—"

"You should know something, Kid."

"Tell me."

"Polignac isn't here just to level Virginia City. He

plans to massacre everyone. Like he did with the citizens of Silver Reef and the pioneers on the trail."

"He won't succeed," I said, indicating the activity all around us. Clemens's newspapers had been distributed and people had been alerted and were angry, grabbing weapons to make a stand against French Rebs at Sun Mountain under the direction of Verbena. Given the mayhem the Confederacy had caused the residents of Virginia City last year, they were eager to seek a measure of retribution. "We know about the sham circus and we discovered the buried cannonballs."

Leaning on his crutches, Foster removed his hat to shield his face from the sun. "Polignac doesn't need cannonballs. He's picked up something even deadlier."

"What's that?"

"Fenian fire."

Some of the miners had shared stories with me in the Blood Nugget about Irish nationalists using white phosphorus against authorities in England and Canada. I'd also read an article about the stuff in the Atlantic and now I wondered if this was what Rosie's peepstone had warned me about.

"All right, then. Come with us, Foster. You're not in fighting condition, but maybe you can offer strategic help."

"Well, sir, I'm a fair shot," he patted the pistol in a holster on his hip, "and I sure as hell ain't afraid." He placed both crutches under one arm and reached to me with the other as I pulled him into the back of the wagon next to Ezra.

Poppy sighed and snapped the reins. Ezra said to Foster, "Kid definitely broke your leg."

Foster laughed. "Actually, he broke my wagon, which ended up breaking my tibia shinbone."

"Yeah, that sounds like Kid."

When we pulled up to the graveyard, it seemed deserted, the only discernible sound—the slow creaking of wood—emanated from an area behind a clapboard structure that was used to store shovels, casket-lowering straps, and other cemetery equipment. Wind whispered through the tombstones like voices of restless ghosts.

Poppy gasped and pointed.

When I looked, the beast within stirred and I knew I couldn't contain it for long.

There, bound to a creaking and slowly spinning Wheel of Death, her eyes wide with fear and pain and mouth gagged, was Sarah. She struggled against the ropes, her scream muffled. But I could see the hope in her eyes, now that Poppy and Ezra and I had come to rescue her.

"Sarah!" Poppy cried.

Before Ezra could hit the brake on the wagon, Poppy jumped off to sprint to the girl.

That's when Ringmaster Clyde stood up from behind a headstone like a malevolent, long-armed scarecrow and grabbed Poppy by the throat before she could raise her gun. She whimpered in his merciless grip.

25

I HOPPED OFF THE WAGON AND WAS ABOUT TO draw my pistol to cut down Clyde with a bullet when I heard the noise of four French mercenaries cocking the hammers on their rifles.

"Don't do it, Kid," one of them growled.

Surrounding me, Ezra, and Foster, the mercs came trudging at us, barrels leveled in our direction.

The sounds sickened me. Frog-eater boots crunching the ground, Poppy's soft moan of agony, Sarah on the creaking Wheel of Death, the grinding screech of the rusted cemetery gate as it swung back and forth in the breeze. Then, amid a silence that suddenly descended on the landscape, a lone figure stood, his silhouette cutting a stark contrast against the bright mountain backdrop.

At the far end of the cemetery, he emerged on horseback, his presence heralded by the glint of sunlight off the saber he held above his head, as if posing for a Gothic painting. I had to admit that he was an impressive sight. Polignac had arrived in full Confederate regalia, a man exuding evil, his twisted grin of confidence sending a shiver down my spine.

He'd come close to snuffing me twice—in Father Ephraim's cavern and Winnie's Silver Reef bedroom. Now he'd try again, this time with additional muscle. As he approached, his black horse seemed to weave between graves like a phantom steed, an animal as graceful as it was lethal.

I gritted my teeth, ready to pull my gun and end them all, yet knowing that when they shot me down, they'd have their way with Poppy, Sarah, Ezra. My heart pounded in my chest as I watched their fate hanging in the balance. As for me, I couldn't have cared less about my end. Dying in a hail of bullets in a Chinese graveyard was as good a sendoff as any. One wrong move, though, meant the difference between the lives of my loved ones...and their deaths.

Polignac stayed on his horse as the animal's face came close to my own, its breath sour and musky. Then the French Reb turned the beast, so he could place the tip of his sword beneath my chin. "After I skewer you, Kid, I'll pulverize your town to rubble."

"Come off your horse," I said, "and fight."

Polignac laughed. "You didn't make out so well last time. Feeling tougher now?"

"Gun him down, Kid," Poppy called. "Even if you win a brawl, they'll shoot us all anyway."

Headlocking my girlfriend with a gun pressed to her spine, Clyde yanked on Poppy's hair to reveal her vulnerable neck, licking it lasciviously as he stared at me with hideous glee. She made a noise of disgust.

Polignac raised his hand, signaling the ringmaster to cease and desist. "You're not without pugilistic skill, Kid. But you're a skinny, immature runt."

"And you're a terrible chess player, on top of being a coward."

That was enough to bring him off his mount. Favoring the leg I'd injured in our cave clash, he removed his belt and scabbard, tossing them to one of his mercs. "Your words will cost you, Kid."

I removed my belt, jacket, and hat. "Ezra," I said and he slowly approached to collect them.

"I'm going to have a 'ball' watching this," he whispered.

I understood his code and gave him authorization. "He's lit my 'fuse.' I'm more than a 'match.'"

As Ezra backed away, and Polignac stepped forward to offer an angled boxing stance, his left hand up and ready to jab, his right pulled to his chest and waiting to throw a hook. His eyes gleamed, predator-like, utterly confident of the outcome.

Our boots shuffled against dry earth as we squared off in a boneyard of buried eternity boxes. The atmosphere crackled with dash-fire menace. It was time to end the conflict.

His first punch hit me like a rail hammer, setting the tone for what I knew would be a brutal spell of pugilism. Emboldened, he surged forward, unleashing a flurry of combinations as I covered up, absorbing most, but not all, of his blows. I wasn't a stranger to pain though, and I managed to move around him, looking for the best angle and countering with a smattering of swift, precise strikes of my own. But it was hard to get past that long straight left. My swing fell short and his straight punch beat my hook every time. Trading jabs with someone of his height, with his reach, was pointless. Polignac also wore a gold ring on his punching hand, which he hadn't removed. It smarted, opening a cut above my eyebrow and drenching my face in blood. It wasn't long before I felt my left ear go wet, knowing it was mangled and that I risked losing it altogether.

He was a clever fighter, but he underestimated my pain threshold.

"Come on, Kid!" Ezra cheered, believing in me even as Polignac picked me apart. "Flatten this bastard!"

"Ezra!" Even with a gun against her back, Poppy couldn't help but scold the boy for his language.

From the periphery of my vision, I saw one of the French Rebs use his rifle to noggin-bop Ezra. "Shut up, runt!"

The shoeshine boy scowled, rubbing his head. And now I was really angry.

Seeing so much gore pouring from my face, Polignac became cocky, show-offish. Rather than snapping and turning over his punches, he let himself follow-through in an effort to wind things up. That was when the monster inside me knew I had him, that he was going to eat dust and lose and die.

Playing opossum, I let him land a terrifying punch that cranked my skull. But I was in a perfect position to bash his face with a spinning backhand that put him down for the count.

"Get up. Get! Up!" I snarled, unable to control the wrath in my voice. "We're not done."

The tide had turned now and I was gratified to see fear in his eyes.

He struggled to stand with stars spinning around his head and I'm sure the injured shinbone did him no favors. He returned to the crouching stance he'd adopted back in Father Ephraim's cave, but this time, he was too wobbly to make it effective. Groggy from the savage hit I'd inflicted, he also forgot to jab, betting everything on his hook. He feinted with his left, slackly, and I instantly saw through it.

"This is for Nellie. You'll never hurt a woman again." I shot out my right hook, beating his own feeble swing.

His legs buckled and he fell face first into the dust. I bent over to taunt him. "Checkmate."

I looked up and saw the French rebels spellbound by the beating of their fearless leader, wondering what to do now. One managed to raise his rifle, swinging it around to aim at me. And that was when Ezra lit the fuse on the cannonball I'd taken from Poppy's opium house and pitch-rolled it in their direction.

The explosion split the heavens, propelling shrapnel that chipped concrete tombstones and eviscerated and decapitated the mercs. Stunned by the sight of Polignac crumpled up on the ground, they'd neglected to monitor Ezra, a cagey boy who'd saved me once before in a sky balloon high above Virginia City.

Ringmaster Clyde, meanwhile, continued to hold Poppy hostage, gun barrel digging into her back as he dragged her through the smoky haze of the detonation toward the buggy. "Don't come near us!" he called. "Or I'll shoot her dead. I swear I will, Kid."

My ears ringing, I watched as Clyde stepped up into the buckboard, jerking Poppy by her throat with one arm, strangling her as she kicked her legs helplessly. He was about to settle into the seat and grab the reins with his gun hand when the unexpected happened.

Foster had snuck into the rear of the wagon and was now using one of his crutches to pin Clyde's arm. He momentarily released Poppy, all she needed to jump off and duck. Clyde, however, grabbed his pistol with his free hand and pointed it behind him to blast Foster point-blank.

Ezra had recovered my Colt and flipped it at me. In slow motion, I saw it hurtling it through the air. I caught it, and aimed at Clyde, just as he drew on me and squeezed off a round. Fortunately for me, it kicked up the dust at my boots.

Unfortunately for him, my round hit its target.

Blood pooled in his chest as he gasped wretchedly and fell off the buggy to writhe and die at Poppy's feet.

"It's all over now," Ezra said to Sarah. "You're safe." Standing on his tiptoes, he removed her mouth gag and undid her bonds on the Wheel of Death, helping her keep her balance. She didn't sob or make a sound.

I ran over to the wagon where Foster lay, clutching the wound in his neck. I removed my shirt to try and stanch it, but it was no good. The artery was ripped apart, jetting blood all over us.

"Foster," I said. "Thank you, from the bottom of my heart. I'm so sorry."

"Don't be," he said. "You saved my life before. Besides, Mama always said…I wasn't good for much…"

"You were good, Foster. A great warrior from Arkansas."

The boy, only five or six years older than Ezra, died in my arms with a final shudder. His death was like that of countless Union and Confederate soldiers in an absurd conflict, a war that I'd left Georgia to avoid, only to be caught up in it here, in a Nevada mining town that Lincoln needed to finance his death machine. Foster's eyes remained open, so I brushed them closed with my swollen pugilist mitt. If there were tears in my eyes, well, they were for myself—not for the dead boy.

Suddenly, a massive barrage of cannon fire erupted from the base of Sun Mountain, where Celestial Circus had set up their carriages, less than a quarter-mile away.

Standing up in the wagon now, I watched plumes of smoke and dirt erupt along C Street, people screaming in horror and anguish, never having thought the war would reach them at the edge of America in a town of mercury-soaked waste and unbridled immorality. But now here they were, scampering for their lives, as cannonballs exploded all around them, wrecking their businesses and homes, reducing their dreams to smoldering debris, blowing apart any chance at a better existence.

And then came the burning white phosphorus shells, raining down on Virginia City with devastating effect. Upon impact, these infernal projectiles ignited with a ferocity that liquefied steel and dissolved flesh to charred remains. Buildings burst into roaring flames, wooden structures engulfed in an inferno that licked at the sky like an insatiable creature from hell. Screams echoed throughout the mountain as men, women, and children fled in terror, clothes, and hair catching fire as they stumbled blindly through choking smoke that misted and melted streets and alleyways.

I turned to say something to Poppy and the kids, but Poppy was already tending to my head wounds and facial lacerations and the rest of the words caught in my throat as I saw who had arrived to join me in counterattacking the cannons.

My Paiute buddy Snake and Nellie the knife thrower and my traveling partner Bad Jace were all riding in the bamboo carriage atop the circus elephant called Hannibal, covered in armor forged at the steelworks in Goblin Valley. Alongside the battle-ready animal stood Rocker the Mormon Enforcer, Elders Wilford and Spencer, and Sister Emma. Samuel Clemens the newspaperman was there with a pistol, as was Verbena the saloon operator, armed with the Hale rocket that we appropriated from

Dr. Skorpion the Medicine Man. Chaparral the piano player and Jericho the bartender stood ready to fight. Ezra and Sarah were in the ranks as well, the latter emitting a shrill whistle that summoned her lion friend. The beast came running from the direction of John John's property.

"Here, Uru!" Sarah called.

"Uru?" It was the first I'd heard the lion's name. "Well, Sarah, I hope Uru is famished and doesn't count French Rebs among his friends."

"None of us do," Rocker said.

"Loyalty to Virginia City always!" Clemens shouted. "Loyalty to the Union only when it deserves it!"

We went charging toward the sound of the cannons, Uru trotting beside Sarah and Hannibal the armor-plated elephant lumbering along with us, like a mythical creature plucked from a Homeric epic.

26

FIVE NAPOLEON CANNONS WERE BOOMING OUT their flat heavy reports, smoke coughing up from their muzzles, and all of them trained on the streets of Virginia City. The noise was so terrifying that my instinct was to seek cover and cower behind the biggest boulder. Being shot at by a cannon turned my insides into gelatin, the oncoming ball making a low sighing sound like a hurricane gathering strength.

The French cannoneers had a decent aim, shells collapsing the Assay Office, the Dead Dice, and the post office. One landed in the bed of a wagon, blasting it to bits, smashing the driver, and injuring the horse. The shriller din was the sound of the animal in agony. Shreds of the wagon were scattered all over the black crater in the ground and some weren't wooden, showing a glistening wetness. The raw rank odor of horse manure filled the air and as the smoke drifted away, we saw that the horse had been cut into two pieces but was still screaming.

Holding my hand, bloodied from the boxing match,

as we ran—against our judgment and inclination—toward the battery, Sarah witnessed the gruesome mess and clenched her jaw, shocked into silence. I knew that she was experiencing something similar to what Poppy had gone through in Canton when the Royal Navy bombarded her city and what Ezra had suffered when his parents were killed by Union guns at Spring Hill Farm. Generation after generation scarred by the madness of war, the senseless deaths of thousands for the satisfaction of tyrants and tycoons. There would be no end to it unless we stopped it here, in a dusty mining town under siege by mercenaries and blasted by cannons of the damned.

Arriving before Hannibal, Rocker and Sarah and I took cover behind an abandoned heap of ore-processing equipment, including a tall roasting-shaft furnace of metal and iron that loomed over us like a threatening pagan entity. We arrived at the side and rear of the French, so the cannoneers didn't spot us as they focused on improving their targeting. I counted thirty Rebs operating the guns, all of them busy with the process of swabbing, reloading, and igniting. None of them had a rifle in hand, but pistols were clearly holstered in the belts.

Crouching, our shoulders pressed against the furnace, Rocker shouted directly into my ear over the cannonade. "We have to hit them now—fast and hard! Let's push Hannibal through their ranks. Then we can pick them off!"

Still shirtless after failing to stop Foster from bleeding out, I said into his own turned ear. "I never liked long-range guns! They're for soldiers who can't fight properly. And they make an awful mess."

"That trip to transport cannons to Kansas doesn't sound impressive now, does it?"

"Not even a tiny bit!"

Hannibal came thundering around the edge of Sun Mountain with Snake. That was when the mercs suddenly realized that they were in for an actual close-up fight.

The towering war elephant trumpeted his elongated nose and stamped his thick columned feet, his massive form casting a long shadow as it shook the ground. The mercs tried to swivel their cannons around to annihilate the animal with phosphorus, but the rocky terrain made it difficult to move the guns and as they barked orders to one another, their voices were drowned out by the rifle fire that Bad Jace and Clemens and Rocker and Elders Wilford and Spencer blasted them with, one of the mercs spinning around in a complete circle before falling down dead in a bloody heap, bullet-punctured.

Several trained their pistols at Hannibal, peppering him with lead-ball rounds. But the Mormons had done such a superb job of covering the animal's vitals with metal plates that he suffered only superficial wounds from the concentrated gunfire. Indeed, Hannibal surged forward like a tidal wave of destruction, unstoppable, his massive bulk trampling everything in his path as he bore down on the enemy, their screams of anguish filling the air as Snake ventilated several more with his Winchester from atop the war elephant. The bone-crushing force of each impact overturned a cannon, men dying beneath the stampeding beast, their bodies breaking and cracking under the relentless advance of a tusked monster that hadn't been outfitted for battle like this since the Roman era. They were, in the end, well-trained soldiers and in an effort to counterattack, they banded together, like gladiators on the floor of the Coliseum, to thrust their bayonets upward like a steel porcupine, seeking to pierce the armor and thick hide of the rampaging beast to bring him crashing to the ground. His trampling momentum was insurmountable, though, and he bowled them over, splintering their bones and stomping them into the rugged terrain of stone and dust.

To make matters worse for them, Bad Jace had brought the Hale rocket tube we'd appropriated from Dr. Skorpion and was in the process of launching it. The weapon was meant for long-distance strikes and was usually angled on a tripod, but I observed now as Bad Jace heaved it onto his shoulder, aiming it—despite its awkward length and unbearable weight—like a rifle. He lost his balance and the barrel began falling until Rocker joined in, helping the man who'd beaten him in an arm-wrestling contest. Indeed, Rocker took it a step further and struck a match to light the fuse. The missile sizzled for a few seconds before shriek-blasting with a sharp sudden propulsion, striking a cannon fifty yards away and shattering its carriage. Another gun neutralized, saving Virginia City from further catastrophe.

Taking advantage of the ensuing lull in the madness, Clemens turned to me while reloading his pistol. "Kid, you've given me so much to write about that I feel indebted."

"Well, I don't wish you boredom, Clemens," I said, watching as Hannibal used his trunk to pick up the rear end of a wagon of escaping mercs to flip it over, the horses rearing back in alarm. "You need to sell newspapers, after all."

Clemens aimed his pistol at a desperate Confederate racing at us with his bayonet, cutting him down with a single shot. "At the very least, I owe you a drink at the

Blood Nugget...as long as it hasn't been flattened by cannons. The worst thing about these French Rebs, I find, is their utter contempt for drinking establishments."

I unloaded my gun into another blade-wielding merc as he tried to sneak up on Bad Jace, who was occupied at that moment with the task of drowning a French Reb in a pool of runoff. At that moment, Clemens was rifle-butted to the ground by someone I didn't anticipate ever getting up again.

There he stood, grinning madly and pointing a carbine at me, his face bruised and battered from the beating I'd inflicted. Otherwise, he remained unscathed by the exploding cannonball that Ezra had detonated in the Chinese graveyard.

"Polignac," I said. "You don't know how to stay dead."

"It's true, I don't," he said, his voice laced with malice, his words twisted from his busted face. "That doesn't mean I can't show *you* how."

"For a nobleman, you sure aren't soft," I said, throwing my empty pistol into the dust.

"I could say the same, plantation prince." He tossed the rifle and came at me fast, eyes aflame with eager demolition, landing a stinging punch to my abdomen.

I recovered quickly, hitting him right in the middle of his big mouth. A good solid blow, with all of the past abuse I'd suffered packed into one punch.

I hit him so hard that I nearly flipped him backward, his boots in the air as he landed with a crunching sound. Polignac lay there for a moment, a dazed expression dancing on his face, his gaze wandering and watery.

I stood over him, waiting for him to regain his senses. I had to admit he was tough. The blow I landed should've put him under for good. "Get up or forfeit. Your choice."

His eyes were clear again as he climbed unsteadily back on his feet. "Ah," he said, with a measure of satisfaction.

I underestimated his speed, however, as he slipped under my next punch, and then he decked me. The next thing I knew, I was on my butt, looking up at him. My head rang, the numbness in my chin spreading to other parts of my jaw, blood dripping from my face again.

Then I rose to my feet slowly and we clobbered each other some more. Out of breath, our limbs drained of strength, we were panting now with every step, every ragged swing, both of us bloody and beyond any notion of a clean victory.

Our fighting, along with the others, seemed to grow static, lethargic, as my friends gathered behind me in support, Polignac's French mercs lining up behind him to witness their commander either triumph or fall at the imminent conclusion of our rivalry.

But accepting a stalemate wasn't in my nature, especially not after all the misery and carnage and slaughter this man had inflicted on my side of the country. I needed to end this—to end Polignac—right now. We staggered on, each throwing drowsy haymakers that never landed, barely able to raise our fists, wanting to knock out the other, but unable to muster the energy after so much exhausted scrapping.

Then, to my horror, I looked past my opponent to see something I couldn't believe. Another cannon being unloaded from a circus wagon, its barrel gleaming in the sun as it rolled down a wooden ramp, its barrel pointed at my friends and me as one of the mercs lit the fuse.

"Hit the dirt!" I yelled.

All of us, including the mercs and Polignac, flattened ourselves in the sand, as the cannon detonated and the ball ripped across the field, from Sun Mountain to downtown Virginia City, exploding the livery where, fortunately, no horses were being sheltered at that time. But the noise and the sight of another devastated landmark in our city was thoroughly demoralizing.

Worse, the destruction seemed to galvanize another wave of fresh mercs, the ones that Polignac had led to our town as they chased me back here. Giddy with violence, the French Rebs came charging at us, at least thirty of them, with bayonets fixed to their rifles, running like electrified demons to bring us to ruin, screaming with vengeance in their hearts, lusting for our blood for having dared defy them in their mission to decimate the source of Lincoln's silver.

"It can't end like this," Poppy said, blood on her face as she helped poor Clemens to his feet. He looked, like all of us, in no shape to resist another assault of ruthless mercs.

"Out of ammo," Bad Jace said, fatigue bringing his voice even lower.

Rocker inspected his rifle, then started searching the muck for dropped cartridges. "I'm done."

No longer riding the frazzled elephant, Snake dragged over a wooden bin of mining water for the dehydrated circus elephant to siphon-scoop with its trunk. "Hannibal can't go on. He's used to performing, not stomping on cannons."

"Kid, we almost beat them," Ezra said without a note of despair. He picked up a bayonet that a French Reb had dropped after getting shot by Rocker, ready to spear the oncoming enemy.

Unable to speak, I pushed over Polignac so that he

fell over into the gore-flecked mud like scarecrow with its stuffing yanked out. Then I picked up my Colt from off the ground, opening the chamber to load it with cartridges, my knuckles split open, my fingers jammed and broken. I spun the chamber, savoring that lovely and comforting sound, before slowly raising the pistol as the screaming mercs came running at full steam.

"To die, to sleep," I said. "Perchance to dream." I cocked the hammer.

Suddenly, there was a bugle call. From the smoke behind us emerged a blue avalanche of at least sixty Union soldiers, hollering at the top of their desert-ravaged lungs. The remnants of Colonel Connor's regiment arrived with a wicked yearning to wallop Confederates, even if they were hired guns from France seeking gold and blood.

Realizing they were slightly outnumbered only seemed to invigorate the mercs. They accelerated their charge, colliding with Connor's troops with a fervor that even I hadn't experienced before. The clang of swords, the popping of pistol and rifle fire, the screams of wounded and dying men. And then things got nasty as the two platoons hacked and slashed and gunned one another to pieces.

I turned to smile at my friends, Nellie stepping forward to embrace me. "Connor showed up!" She smiled at me and kissed my cheek. "The little Irishman saved us again!"

As I reciprocated her caress, I saw that Polignac had drawn a knife from his boot and was hurling it straight at Nellie's back. "Traitorous bitch!" he called out.

I shoved her aside in time, but the blade found my ribs, lodging deep. I fell to my knees, bright pain behind my eyes, my vision tunneling.

"Kid!" Nellie said, placing her hand on the handle of the knife, but hesitating to pull it out.

"Don't let Scully near me," I said, my lips numbing. "Just put me in one of Grover's coffins."

I watched helplessly as Polignac drew another throwing weapon. But then Sarah was standing close to him and he said, "Little girl, care to watch your town hero's demise?"

"I'm watching yours," she answered calmly.

Uru leaped so fiercely that Polignac didn't have a chance to scream, his throat instantly ripped out by the lion's savage jaws. He twitched for only a moment as the animal feasted.

I watched with some pleasure until I lost consciousness.

27

I awoke in a satin-lined coffin the next day, all of my limbs intact thanks to Poppy, who kept Dr. Scully away. She allowed only Grover to work on me as he cleaned my wound—no vitals nicked—and stitched me up and saved me yet again from death. Unfortunately, he wasn't able to do the same for a score of townspeople who'd succumbed to cannon and Fenian fire.

I had more than a few visitors over the next few days, mainly from the Mormon steelworks community of Goblin Valley, including dear and delightful little Dolly, who seemed to thrive in a society where family was a priority. Emma came every day with a plate of food, usually from the oven of Winnie, doing a land-office business in pasties, as Poppy was too busy helping other residents of Virginia City to rebuild their damaged storefronts, especially Verbena. The beautiful saloon operator lost the Dead Dice, but soon recruited Chaparral and Jericho to remove debris and start framing a new structure for their employer. She had the good sense to pay them in liquor and gambling credits.

Rocker and Bad Jace buried the arm-wrestling hatchet, and it was nice to see two deadly outlaws behave courteously to each other, though I mostly credited the schoolteacher, Lydia Sweet, for improving their personalities. She was a beacon of light in a town that generated darkness and grime, and I felt silly for having misjudged an educator, even if I had no desire to see how well Bad Jace had done decorating her classroom.

After killing a number of them, Colonel Connor encouraged the mercs to surrender, placing them under arrest, trying them for insurrection and sabotage, and shipping them to a federal prison in Arizona Territory, where I assumed they'd be exchanged for favors from the French government—such as maintaining neutrality and ceasing to help the Confederate army.

More significantly, Connor ended up prying a piece of significant information from them—namely, the location of the missing gold from Ephraim's cave, which Ralston indicated was a relief to Lincoln.

The cannons that Rocker and his Mormons forged for the Union arrived in time for a major battle in Arkansas, resulting in a military victory for the president. I thought about poor Foster and, though I tried later to find his body, there was too much lime in the graveyard and I had to give up and settle for writing his parents a letter, telling them that their son was, at least in my eyes, a hero who had rescued me and Poppy and Ezra from certain death.

Dr. Skorpion the Medicine Man hit the road again, selling his patented elixirs to mercury-poisoned miners from Nevada to New Mexico.

As for Nellie, I never saw her again, although I thought of her often for many years after. She was an incredible warrior and someone who loved as fiercely as she fought. I did, however, receive a telegram from her once, that arrived shortly after Poppy and I were married in Virginia City. The message read:

DEAR KID,
CONGRATS.
WISH I WAS THERE TO CELEBRATE.
THINK OF YOU OFTEN.
RAN INTO YR DAD IN BATON ROUGE.
INTERESTING FELLOW.
HE IS ON HIS WAY TO VC.
BE CAREFUL KID.
I LOVE YOU.
NELLIE

WATCH FOR: STAGECOACH TO OBLIVION (KID CRIMSON 3)

AVAILABLE SEPTEMBER 2024

ABOUT THE AUTHOR

Jarret Keene is an assistant professor in the Department of English at UNLV, where he teaches American literature and the graphic novel. He is the series editor for Las Vegas Writes, published by Huntington Press, and is the author of *Hammer of the Dogs*, and the middle grade books *Decide and Survive: The Attack on Pearl Harbor* and *Heroes of World War II: 25 True Stories of Unsung Heroes Who Fought for Freedom*. Keene has been interviewed by *Writer's Digest*, *Publisher's Weekly*, *EcoTheo Review*, *Library Thing*, *Black Fox Literary Magazine*, and Coast to Coast AM.